CAREER SUICIDE!

CONTEMPORARY LITERARY HUMOUR

CAREER SUICIDE!

CONTEMPORARY LITERARY HUMOUR

EDITED BY JON PAUL FIORENTINO

WITH AN INTRODUCTION BY DAVID MCGIMPSEY

LIVRES
DC
BOOKS

Moosehead Anthology #9: Contemporary Literary Humour
Edited by Jon Paul Fiorentino

Design by conundrum

First edition. Printed in Canada

National Library of Canada Cataloguing in Publication

The Moosehead anthology.

Annual.
[No. 1]-
Continues: Moosehead review.
ISSN 0842-1765
ISBN 0-919688-69-1 (issue 9)

1. Canadian literature (English)—20th century—Periodicals.
2. Literature, Modern—20th century—Periodicals. 3. Canadian literature (English)—21st century—Periodicals. 4. Literature, Modern—21st century—Periodicals.

PS8233.M66 1988-   C810'.8'0054   C89-039024-X
PR9194.4.M66 1988-

DC Books gratefully acknowledges the suport of The Canada Council for the Arts and of SODEC for our publishing program.

 Canada Council for the Arts **Conseil des Arts du Canada**

DC BOOKS / LIVRES DC
Box 662, 950 Decarie, Montreal, Quebec, H4L 4V9, Canada

CONTRIBUTORS

Introduction by David McGimpsey   6

Editor's Note by Jon Paul Fiorentino   11

Robert Allen   13

Ryan Arnold   19

Joe Blades   26

Andy Brown   28

Stephen Cain   38

Jason Camlot   41

Margaret Christakos   48

Jon Paul Fiorentino   52

Corey Frost   54

Valerie Joy Kalynchuk   57

Ryan Kamstra   60

David McGimpsey   65

rob mclennan   69

Nathaniel G. Moore   71

Eva Moran   76

Hal Niedzviecki   80

Mark Paterson   87

Jamie Popowich   100

Robert Priest   104

Stuart Ross   106

Victoria Stanton   111

Sarah Steinberg   115

Anne Stone   119

Todd Swift   126

Julia Tausch   129

Sherwin Tjia   133

Paul Vermeersch   139

Sheri-D Wilson   143

DAVID McGIMPSEY

INTRODUCTION
FROM SEA TO SHINY MANAGEABLE HAIR

Contemporary *Canadian* literary humour? I'm laughing already!

Unless one is talking about some tasty bacon, you have to admit "Canadian" is not the greatest adjective in the advertising world. Given Canadian literature's reputation for high earnestness, for novels that start out with ten-page descriptions of family farms in the London, Ontario region, for poems that start out with ten-page descriptions of family farms in the London, Ontario region, Canadian literary humour may sound like one of those "wondrous strange" rarities—like *Shaquille O'Neal's Greatest Hits* or a gourmet Scottish restaurant. I would go as far as to say that high earnestness has become the commercial brand of Canadian literature, and while there's lots of good product in that line, the main body of Canadian Literature generally sees humour as marginal, or antithetical to dominant literary strategies which seek to define the Canadian as something obviously important and seriously different than the American.

Wherever, artistic social circles often seek to define themselves as *serious* and this has not only led to an inordinate ratio of beret-wearing at poetry readings vs. beret-wearing at NASCAR events, but a reluctance to recognize the comedic within the same breath as the serious. Mark Twain always fretted about writing a novel that would be taken seriously, Woody Allen's transformation from stand-up comedian to auteur is a long study in the public performance of seriousness and that guy who played Urkel—where's his Peabody Award? Of course, as any casual observer of the Academy Awards knows, comedies never win for best picture. However, if a movie was made about a one-armed trombonist who sublimates his love for Tom Cruise by composing concertos for a one-legged woman played by Penelope Cruz, there'd be a better chance for institutional recognition—even more so if the protagonist was played by Ralph Fiennes and the Cruise and Cruz parts were played by Meryl Streep and Joseph Fiennes.

Humour, of course, tends to mock earnestness and pretension, much like Cher mocked Sonny. Jokes consistently subvert seemingly good intentions by revealing a less noble nature in a shared failed humanity. Humour avails itself to the people and often overrides other discourses with one simple but ruthless standard: *if people laugh, it is funny.* Jerry Lewis, in a startling interview where he asserts his lack of book-reading skills could prepare him for the science of brain surgery better than most, also said, in the end, the comedian must get the laughs, regardless of the quality of the laugh. The comedic writer or the humourist (a term I imagine intended to alleviate the stress put on the comedian to be funny—I mean, if many of today's columnists are an example, humourists apparently don't have to be that funny) can be as skilled and as studied as the most grave of authors, but they have to be willing to be thought of as *unserious*—as humourists as opposed to writers. Humour punctures the politician's quest for respect, skewers the celebrity's regal stature, and shreds the intellectual's pomp. Often drawing towards deeply-held suspicions about the way of the world, the humourist ultimately falls on her or his own sword and dares not yell "ouch." For example, a literary scholar may welcome knowing the term *bildungsroman* as a way of saying "coming of age story"; a comedian may understand the phrase, but may not be able to resist mocking its pretentious sound. You can simply forget about *kunstleroman*.

One of the problems with a sense of humour is everybody believes they have one. While people are not at all shy in admitting "I'm not a good dancer," or "I'm not a very good squash player," few will say, even when there's compelling evidence, "I don't have a sense of humour." To admit to having no sense of humour would be to admit to a catastrophic failure of personality. I have a theory that goes when people boast "I like all kinds of music!" what they really mean is "I like Fleetwood Mac, especially *Rumours*." Similarly, when people say they like funny things they usually mean they like what they like. Senses of humour are all so different: not everybody laughs themselves sick watching reruns of *The A-Team*, some do not spend good portions of their spare time perfecting their impressions of Moe the Bartender.

Given the highly subjective nature of comedy, comedic failure is often perceived as a fault of the artist. Someone might say to a poet: "I didn't understand your poem about the asthmatic Bishop—it was too dense and I needed to look a few things up" but, to a comedian they might say "I didn't laugh at all at your bit about the asthmatic Bishop. It stunk—you suck!" Admittedly, the audience shifts every which way and we find different communities of humour: Sam Kinison might not have gone over well as a guest on *The Prairie Home Companion*; Garrison Keillor's unlikely to play "Stump the Homeless" on *The Howard Stern Show*. Often when one finds opposition to the most determined anti-intellectual humourists like Dice Clay or Don Cherry, their critics try to assure us these people are actually "not funny"; their defenders in turn say the critics have "no sense of humour."

When David Sedaris read one of his stories at a podium on the stage of the David Letterman show, and *killed* in the way a good stand-up would, I thought it showed a welcome literary maturation; at least one author had "caught up" to a comedic standard defined by television, where people have become used to comedy that is fast and layered joke upon joke. Naturally, this approach might not be welcome news in bookish circles where the phrase "but, I don't even own a television!" is frequently intoned as if it was the proud announcement of a vow of cultural chastity. Even if admitting you don't have a TV sort of sounds like saying "but I never heard of shampoo!" or "you eat toast?" But, in comedy, as well as literature, people find humour where they want to find it. For fans of science fiction, Phillip K. Dick is wonderfully wry; for fans of Carrot Top, seeing Carrot Top live is sublimely hilarious; many assume that guy at their workplace who does that impression of Bob Cole is "the funniest guy ever." Suicidal poet John Berryman was noted for his wit and, who knows, maybe in certain circles it's Sylvia "Slappy" Plath and Robert "Shecky" Lowell.

To be a funny writer may have certain risks, but it is a risk many delight in. Considering how many writers decide to write sad tales about defeated fathers in undershirts, dedicating one's self to actually making people laugh has many sweet rewards. American poet Matt Mason succinctly sums dangers of being a funny literary artist in his poem "The Funny Poet Renounces Funny Poetry and Concentrates on Making the World a Better, More Beautiful Place (in Which He Has Sex More Often)":

> "I like being funny, it's a compliment, but (…) not always the compliment I'm fishing for. (I)t just means you're not taken seriously. You're the Moon Pie on the dessert tray of the black tie dinner at that snooty French restaurant (…) you've got an arrow through your head as the poet laureate floats past in a smog of tweed."[1]

I would say the "smog of tweed" gets quite dense in Canada, and even considering Canadian success in film and TV comedy, the national smog alert gets higher and higher. Luckily there's always more beyond the commercial brand of Canadian literature, even if its high earnestness is found in the patter of a cross-eyed formalist or a pining spoken-worder—funny poems and stories flourish just beside this productive frame. Perhaps this is not surprising considering poems and stories often start out being read to small audiences where laughter remains the only quantifiable response. That is to say, at book readings, few people leap up to say "wonderful simile!" or "a magnificent doppelganger for the protagonist, read on!" Of course, if the artist strings together a few funny pieces in a row, he or she should be prepared to answer the question: "have you ever thought of going into stand-up comedy?"

---

[1] Mason, Matt. "The Funny Poet Renounces Funny Poetry …" *The Green Mountains Review.* 15, 1-2, 152-53.

I realize there's nothing as unfunny as trying to analyze humour, except maybe whatever show NBC currently has scheduled after *Friends*. Whatever subversive energies it may possess, humour is also an instinctively trusted measure of communication, a truth-revealing way of conceding human fault. Funnies are a constant part of all literary experience and, whatever middlebrow fussiness associated with current Canadian literary exercise, a beloved part of the Canadian literary tradition. The great names of Canadian literary humour are all well known and, to no surprise, none of these great artists have spent time telling crowd-pleasing jokes that end with the punchline "moose cock." Well, maybe Frederick Philip Grove—but no one else!

From what I've skimmed, *Career Suicide* is a collection of a new generation of funny-talkers. Poems and stories which find their laughs in different quarters: in the wry, the slapstick, the satiric and the dark. If this collection is any indication, one of the characteristics of contemporary Canadian literary humour may well be its engagement with popular culture. In this collection the importance of *DKNY*, Corey Feldman, *Lik M Aid*, Randy Savage, John Cougar Mellancamp, the game of *Clue*, all begin to take on a status which, I think, questions the limiting purview of what may be deemed "serious." Perhaps there's something in the way the popular intercedes against loftier cultural ambitions—you know, the way no one will read your poetry because they'd prefer to listen to *Rumours*.

From Ryan Arnold's Olympic Stadium to Jason Camlot's Taj Mahal, the authors in this collection construct works of art based on the world that is actually in front of them. As odd and off-putting and hilarious as that may be—the authors in this collection find their laughs, as we all do, in the limitations of human experience and, one suspects, pre-mixed *mai tais*. Their virtues as "serious" writers are so obvious, to maintain more argument about literary humour would be a kind of career suicide. While many of the authors in this collection are probably patriotic enough, I think, with great excitement, this collection at least doesn't feel, to me, exclusively *Canadian*.

O Canada: so many funny writers! So many people who, after the serious and award-winning writers rejected appeals to appear in this journal, were ready to step into the breach.

I kid! I joke! I love Frederick Philip Grove!

JON PAUL FIORENTINO

EDITOR'S NOTE

Look, I'll level with you. I don't "get" jokes. Humour makes me feel uncomfortable, sad and sometimes itchy. But you see, despite my inability to understand anything comedic, I have put together this very funny book, written by funny people who consistently "make with the funny." The truth is I needed some money and literary publishing is full of suckers. DC Books, the publisher of this book, has no idea that I am actually not the esteemed poet and literary starlet, Jon Paul Fiorentino, but in fact, Nino Torres, a cross-dressing Cuban refugee with no formal education and a penchant for glow-bowling. Ah, the sweet, sweet power of editing—it's tasty like diabetic candy. I haven't read much of the book but I assure you of its quality. The authors collected here were found in various swingers clubs throughout upstate New York and the tri-state area. This book is truly a Canadian treasure, like Walt Whitman or Kenny Rogers or the great sport of lawn darts. I'm bored. And now, for no reason, please enjoy the following sketch which I drew all by myself:

And, as you may have guessed, that little boy grew up to be Ed Begley Jr. Now, sit back, relax and take off your pants. It's go time.

ROBERT ALLEN

BLUE-EYED DOCTOR

She was newly engaged, and already eyeing
blue-eyed doctor sperm, which she saw advertised
on a late night infomercial.

June Cleaver pearls are part of the whole retro fit
along with plastic picket fencing, maintenance free,
and a clubby martini with friends, at a downtown club.

She's unhappy, and hungry for love, which
she imagines comes with DKNY clothes
and a body cleansed with bottled oils and water.

No man could give her all this, least of all her
high-tech husband, who turns every night in the
mirror, watching pecs and six-pack dissolve like soap.

But the night is as brutal black as it ever was
when the lights go out. The two are as much of the
natural world as grass, about to go under the scythe.

When they have children it is ten times worse.
The children, despite being born in a prison, are
happy and bright. Two are utterly conventional.

One is a blue-eyed doctor who kills at night.

THE NATURAL HISTORY OF ERROL FLYNN'S COCK

Marilyn Monroe took the freight elevator
from the first to the third floor of the Watergate Hotel.

Jack was there in sunglasses, and she told him
she'd heard Errol Flynn play "You are my sunshine"

with his cock on an ordinary piano, on an ordinary
night in Hollywood, with the burning stars

rigid with sameness through the smoke,
and it was like Egypt two thousand years before

when Cleopatra was delivered in a carpet to Julius
Caesar, and unrolled at his feet, and it was like

a sorrowing and fat Orson Welles, who drank
to get the Third Man theme to take leave of his head,

while his liver settled like ice on the moon.
Jack laughed like a boy, clear off his philandering head,

and she told him about Lauren Bacall, leaning
against the door, her face lit with unhappiness.

Bogey would leave her, or someone for her,
descending into hell with the hands of the clock.

Bogey was smoking a private brand, with two gold rings,
no filter. This was before most of us were born,

but after the Mayans and dinosaurs and Lucy of Africa.
I sometimes claim to have been there in the freight elevator

at the Watergate Hotel, to hear Jack Kennedy get
Marilyn's account of Errol Flynn's cock. (It is hard, even for me,

to believe it.) And that I filmed them on Super-8,
paying overmuch attention to Marilyn.

What is certain is that a tear-shaped singularity
filled the camera eye, and those same

immutable stars hadn't drifted an inch
so far as human time could tell. Errol Flynn's

cock still bangs the keys like a virtuoso, though
Errol's gone, like Marilyn, Bogey, Kennedy, Jim Dean

and all. They rub bare shoulders with Lucy of Africa,
waiting for Bacall, each alone as Garbo, in her own

small cleft. And it was Errol's cock sang "You are my
Sunshine," on an upright piano, once upon a time.

A POEM AND A DIME WILL NO LONGER BUY YOU A CUP OF COFFEE

Look out on Shuter Street—there are two hundred
people down there, mostly going through garbage cans.
They won't find much in mine.

All the way downtown I bounced off panhandlers,
arriving broke at the ferry docks. There I recited
my latest work, based on a random profusion
of liquid sounds: elk language for the existential mob.

Not a thin dime came from this, though a mime came up
and appeared to produce a five dollar bill from my ear.

Next time I will bring my dwarf. He sings arias
and old ladies weep.

But I cannot cash tears—tears won't pay the rent.
Back on Shuter Street meanwhile, someone has ripped
off my garbage can, and my typewriter hasn't written

a thing since I went out.
I curse capitalism, as does my dwarf.

Every night, at a friend's suggestion, I stay up late
to see something he calls rosy-fingered dawn.

My friend and I both have literary backgrounds,
as does my dwarf, who rescues comic books that smell
of ash and apples and porkrind

from the garbage cans on Shuter Street,
and never anything good to eat.

At Mickey's tavern they've raised the price of beer
by a nickel. "It's an economic boom for me, these

bad times," he says.

But that's okay—because of inflation
the magazines I contribute to now give me three free
copies instead of two.

Me and my dwarf and my typewriter are starving.
I could have gone on the dole, but when I said I was a
poet they said I could never be unemployed, ever,
and when my dwarf said "dwarf" they threw us both out.

I usually sleep until four in the afternoon
when my dwarf brings me the morning paper
and together we read the want ads.

My dwarf is getting surly.
I remind him I am listed in *The Directory of American Poets*
and ask if he'll hold a spot for me in the soup line.

He throws *The Directory of American Poets* at me
and snarls "Eat that, you son of a bitch."

Outside the same two hundred people are still
going through the garbage cans, sounding like
the world's worst band from Trinidad.

My dwarf goes to join them, with that
eurotrash sneer he has, in mock deference
to my PhD—my dwarf never got out of high school.
He couldn't reach the door handle.

I once sold some poems to *The New York Times*.
Twenty-five dollars each! Now every time I meet
someone named Sulzberger I shake his hand
and my dwarf sings him an aria.

DON'T LET JULIA FOOL YA, THO' SHE'S FROM PUMPKINVILLE...

— Canada is Satan's sperm bank
  (Fred Phelps, U.S. Evangelist)

She was nice as two cherries, and talk was balm
from her lips. Till she got on to religion, and I
was shocked. It was a narrow path, she said,
flanked by thorn plants of the sort her
saviour ate for breakfast, then wore on his
head. I'm in town to kick Satan's ass, she said,
bright as day and pretty as god's flowerpots.
Then with a tongue that licked redly
on Canadian air, she linked arms with god
for a tour of Satan's lot, and left me high and
dry. So many women with the wrong guy.

RYAN ARNOLD

THE BIG HURT

Paul eased himself into one of the kitchen chairs, with his hairless, stumpy calves exposed beneath his stolen Hyatt robe. He scratched at the bits of toilet paper and traces of shaving cream stuck in the folds of his neck. He looked at the wall and then at the calendar. Travis' birthday. Thirty-seven.

Travis walked into the kitchen. "Would you like some grapefruit," Paul asked.

"Okay," Travis said. "No sugar."

Paul walked over to the fridge and pulled out two grapefruit halves, carefully sliced the night before. He put each halve onto a plate and sprinkled both with a tiny spoonful of sugar. He took a second spoonful and mounded his with a pile that reminded him of a tiny toboggan slope.

"Happy birthday," Paul said. He rubbed his hand on Travis' forehead. He placed the plates on the table. "Thirty-seven, I can hardly believe it. Dig in."

"Thanks," Travis said. He pulled the sleeve of his Duke University sweat shirt over his fist, and rubbed his hairline. Travis hated it when Paul touched the top of his head, and in his mind, made light of his stout, four-foot-seven frame.

Travis scratched his testicles and opened the sports section. They ate breakfast in silence. Travis was upset and realized that Paul had added some sugar to his grapefruit. Travis wasn't supposed to eat sugar, but he understood why Paul did it. Paul loved sugar and he loved the sweet taste. To him, sugar was like love itself.

When he finished, Paul stood up and made a remark about Frank Thomas' 0 for 5 game the previous night against the Tigers, stretching a career high slump to 0 for 28. Paul placed his plate in the sink. Travis was a huge Frank Thomas fan and was obviously aggravated by the remark.

"Listen," Travis said, "when Montreal has a Triple Crown threat first baseman, like the Big Hurt, just let me know. Then, and only then, will we talk about 0 for fucking 5." Frank Thomas' nickname, *The Big Hurt*, was, in Travis' opinion, the best nickname in the world of sport. He repeated it often, and in the eyes of Paul, grossly overused it.

Paul didn't respond. He left the kitchen and went down the hallway to get ready for work. He knew that when he said anything about Frank Thomas, or anything about African American athletes, Travis took it very seriously. Sometimes, like that morning, he got exceptionally upset. Sometimes his behavior made Travis feel sorry for Paul, but most of all, it made him feel sorry himself.

It was golf shirt Friday at Paul's office, so getting prepared took less time than usual. Normally he spent the extra few minutes on Fridays talking to Travis about baseball, but he knew he'd crossed the line. He had really upset Travis and he'd wait until later, at the Expos' game, to assess the damage. Until it was time to leave, he sat on their laundry hamper in the bedroom, almost collapsing the weak plastic sides with his mass.

At 8:10, he left without saying goodbye, wearing his only golf shirt—a blue Greg Norman, with a white shark's-tooth pattern around the collar. The shirt had been a gift from Travis last year, on Paul's thirty-fifth birthday.

That night, Paul met Travis at the Metro station. The air was hot and humid. As they rode the train, they both perspired. It was crowded. They had to stand.

They arrived at the stadium gates about 30 minutes before game time. They decided they'd go down to field level to see if they could get any Expo autographs. Much to their disappointment, Montreal had already left the field and it was the shit Padres taking batting practice.

"Fucking hell," Paul said, looking at Fred McGriff shagging grounders down on the field.

"That's too bad," Travis said. "Maybe we'll be able to get some after the game."

"Yeah," Paul replied. "Maybe."

Paul thought about apologizing to Travis, but in the end, he decided not to. Anyway, Travis was probably busy thinking about Frank Thomas belting homers in the game against Detroit at New Comisky Park. "3 for 4 with four RBIs," Paul thought, "that would show him."

After a while they looked at each other.

"You look nice in that golf shirt," Travis said. "It fits perfectly."

"Thank you," Paul replied. "Let's go to the seats. I'm tired of standing."

They walked up the ramp to the upper level of the stadium where they sat in their usual seats on the third base line. Their season ticket seats were in the first row of the upper level of the stadium. They liked these because they had no one blocking their view and because they could rest their sodas on the cement ledge in front of them. Sometimes, when the Expos were losing, Travis dropped pieces of popcorn down on the spectators in the lower level. They'd look over the ledge and laugh at the reactions of the people below. It was the sort of thing that kept them interested when the games were boring or there was a long pause when a new pitcher was warming up. By the time they sat down, the stadium was pretty much empty. It was still early.

"I can't believe the crowds we've been getting lately," Paul said. "Even in a play-off race, we only had eleven thousand last night."

"I know," replied Travis. "I think it's because of the strike rumors."

"That's kooky-talk," Paul said.

"They said in the paper today that it's almost a sure thing. They're going on strike."

"Fucking greedy owners," Paul said. "Who do they think they are?" They both shook their heads, and looked at the advertisements flashing on the screen. "Bastards."

"I wrote a poem today," Travis said.

"You did? Is it good?"

"I wrote it for you."

"Can I hear it?" Paul asked.

"Sure."

Travis smiled, and pulled out a tiny piece of paper from his pocket. He cleared his throat. "It's titled, 'Paul'… *I love you, you love me / we'll go to the sugar tree / there will be bees / and there will be sugar / but the bees won't sting, / they'll be more interested in the sugar / and we won't bother them / because our love is sweeter than sugar.*"

When he finished reading, Paul had his glasses off. He scratched his eye. Travis mistook this as a signal that Paul had really been moved. But Paul knew almost nothing about poetry. He didn't even know what was good and what was bad. But he thought this poem probably wasn't a good one. It didn't matter. Also, he thought he'd heard it somewhere before.

"It's nice," Paul said. He coughed, and spat something onto the ground. "Let's watch the game."

"But it hasn't started yet," Travis said.

"I know."

The field was clearing after warm-up and the crowd was slowly starting to fill the seats around home plate.

"I love you," Travis said as the groundskeepers came out from behind the right field wall.

"Let's watch the game," Paul replied. The groundskeepers began working on the infield. Paul put his glasses in his pocket and stared at the field. They sat in silence for 20 minutes, until the Expos finally took the field, at which point they both stood and applauded louder than they ever had before.

The game was great. They drank sodas, ate nachos, but most of all, they cheered. They had a wonderful night, and the memory of the argument rarely entered their minds. Travis even drank a beer to celebrate his birthday. It was wonderful. By the bottom of the eighth inning, the Expos were leading 4 to 1. They had a runner in scoring position, and Larry Walker was up. He had already hit a single, a double, and a triple. Walker had driven in two runs, but more importantly, was just a home run away from the cycle. He worked the count full, and then he dug in for the pitch—a sure fastball. The crowd of sixty-five hundred fans rose to their feet, sensing something great was about to happen. Trevor Hoffman delivered the ball, and Walker took a huge cut. At that moment, Paul envisioned the ball flying off the bat, and sailing into the empty right field bleachers. But what happened next was a surprise to everyone. Walker swung slightly behind the pitch, popping it into foul territory. When it reached its peak, Paul noticed that the ball was dropping in their direction. He hit Travis on the arm, and they jumped onto their seats, poising their mitts in anticipation of a souvenir. As the ball fell, Paul felt a rush of adrenaline like never before.

The ball was dropping fast, and Paul sensed he could reach it. But, as it came closer, he thought back to his little league days when a ground ball hit him in the groin, forcing the embarrassing end of his athletic career. Paul thought back to that pain, and withdrew his glove. The ball flew past him, and just when it seemed out of reach, he saw it drop into Travis' Frank Thomas mitt. Paul jumped up, and threw his hands into the air. He was so excited, he didn't even see Travis, leaning well over the railing, fall over the overhang. A second later Paul gasped, while in slow motion, Travis fell two stories down to the cement stairway below. The crowd, who had momentarily cheered the great catch, stood in awe.

To Paul, there seemed to be no sound when Travis hit the ground. So, when he finally looked over the railing, he expected a fan below had either broken the fall, or else caught Travis in his or her arms. But when he looked down, all he could see was the ball planted firmly in the pocket of the mitt, and Travis' blood pooling on the stairs between the shoes of grade six classmates on a field trip from Ste.-Adèle. In the chaos, Pierre-Alexandre, a nearby vendor, dropped his tray of lukewarm Labatt 50, and screamed "Tabernac-encore." The beer splashed everywhere while an unflappable Larry Walker walked back to the Expos dugout to get a new bat. Meanwhile, the golden Labatt streamed down the stairs until it was dammed by Travis' body, the bitter liquid soaking into his Duke sweatshirt.

There was no funeral for Travis. He didn't have any family or friends other than Paul. It seemed inappropriate for Paul to hold a memorial service for him since he was sure no one would come. Paul could've invited one of his co-workers, but he didn't really want any of them to know about Travis. What Paul did do was agree to a proposal made by a woman in the public relations department of the Montreal Expos. She called Paul on the phone a few days after the accident to suggest they hold a brief memorial service before the Expos' next home game against the San Francisco Giants. She asked if Paul would come out onto the field, say a few words, and then throw the first pitch after a moment of silence. The woman said the accident had shocked and touched everyone who had been at the game. She also said that Larry Walker had said it was a real shame that Travis died, and he wished that he hadn't been the one who'd hit the foul ball. Paul thanked her for the opportunity to honor his friend.

"You've got lots of time to prepare something," the woman said. "The team's on a thirteen game West Coast road-trip."

"Great."

On the afternoon of the game, Paul entered the stadium through a special door reserved for players and media. There was a tired-looking guard at the door.

"Paul Miles," he said to the man. He glanced at his clipboard.

"Right through there," he said, pointing to a small area enclosed by a blue curtain. "Wait in there, and someone will come get you."

When the time came, Paul walked out onto the field without noticing the players in the dugout, or the almost eight-thousand fans who were waiting for the game to start—the opener of perhaps the final series of a strike-shortened season. Paul took the mound, just like the lady had told him to do, and stood at the microphone.

"Good evening everyone," he said after the feedback subsided. "I'm here today to say goodbye to a very good friend of mine. He passed away here at Olympic Stadium during an Expos game, not even three weeks ago today. His name was Travis Hardaway. Some might think that his life was tragic, and so his death was fitting, but I wish he was still here today. I loved him and I just wanted to say a few words." Paul raised the microphone stand. He said, "*Travis, I love you, you love me / we'll go to the sugar tree / there will be bees / and there will be sugar / but the bees won't sting, / they'll be more interested in the sugar / and we won't bother them / because our love is sweeter than the sugar.*" Paul paused, and looked into the stands. "Goodbye," he said.

"Thank you very much," a man in an umpire's uniform said. "And to honour Mr. Hardaway, we are pleased to announce that the Moffats are going to sing "O Canada." Then, four young teenage boys in Toronto Blue Jays jerseys stepped onto the field and began singing the national anthem, *toute en anglais*.

"But Travis was American," Paul said into the microphone. The umpire looked at him, but it hadn't been on and, of course, no one had heard him. When the song was over, the crowd applauded, and Darrin Fletcher ran out to the mound and handed Paul an official Major League baseball.

"Throw the first pitch," he said.

Paul waited for Darrin Fletcher to get into his catching stance behind the plate. Then, he went into the stretch, and threw the ball as hard as he could. He imagined it was the same ball that had killed Travis. He threw it hard, like he never wanted to see it again. The ball flew right over the plate, about four inches from the dirt. It made a snap as it hit Darrin Fletcher's glove.

When it was over, the lady showed Paul off the field through the Expos dugout. They were making their way into the tunnel, when Felipé Alou asked Paul if he wanted to watch the game from the Expos bench.

"I heard you're a big ball fan," Felipé said.

"Yes I am, Mr. Alou," Paul replied.

"Call me coach. Here, put on this batting helmet and have a seat with the guys on the bench. That was some poem."

By the ninth inning, Montreal was down by a run, and up to bat. Paul thought about Travis and how excited he would've been to see him in the Expos dugout. He smiled.

"Hey there, partner," a man said as he sat down beside Paul. "A real nail biter, eh?" Paul turned to face the man. It was Larry Walker.

"It sure is," Paul replied.

"Call me Larry. Hey, that was a nice pitch you threw out there today. You've got a decent arm."

"Yeah, I wanted to play ball when I was younger, but I didn't have much speed on the base path, or general athletic ability. Plus, I was hit in the groin with a hard grounder."

"Well, it wasn't a bad pitch at all. A little low, but right down the middle. And hard. Just a touch low."

"It wasn't low," Paul said. "I mean, it may have been low for you or me, but Travis was a shorter fellow, and if he was at the plate, it would have been right in his wheelhouse. A strike, right at the knees." Paul turned away from Larry Walker and looked out at the field.

"Yeah," Larry said, "life's a bitch."

"I don't know," Paul said. "It's not so bad sometimes."

Larry didn't know what to say. He wanted to say sorry for hitting the ball that killed Travis. He wanted to tell him that he was right, life wasn't such a bitch. He wanted to say that sometimes, life is pretty damn sweet. He also wanted to ask him if he was authorized to be sitting in the dugout. But he didn't.

24

"I don't know," Larry said, "I think most umps would agree that it was a little low. What do you think Darrin, a little low?"

Darrin Fletcher shrugged his shoulders.

"You don't understand," Paul said. "It was right in his wheelhouse. It was perfect. Low, hard, and right at the knees. He would've flared that baby right up the middle. Or a bunt single. A bunt single at least."

Just then, Marquis Grissom, the Expos' last out, swung at strike two. As Rod Beck got ready to throw the pitch, Paul stood up and handed his helmet to Larry Walker.

"You won't need one of these again tonight," he said.

Larry didn't say anything. He looked on as the Giants' closer blew strike three past Grissom's bat, just inches above the plate. Walker threw the helmet. "Goddamn it," he said.

As Paul stood at the entrance of the tunnel, he saw that Larry was looking at him. Momentarily, Paul thought about Travis. He thought about the pending strike. Travis would've played for free, he thought. Paul felt blood rushing to his face. He was angry.

"Hey," Larry said. "You can't go in there."

Then, just before Paul turned down the tunnel, he looked right into Larry Walker's eyes. "Motherfucker," he yelled, turning quickly and sprinting toward the clubhouse.

JOE BLADES

TRANS-CANADA MEDITATION

Rocky Horror Poetry Show

In just seven days ... I can make you a manuscript

Come up to the lab... and see whats on the slab...

ANDY BROWN

THE ANDY BROWN PROJECT

Who is Andy Brown?

Well, according to my dad, I'm a lazy, long-haired layabout. This is partly true, having recently spent 2 years learning how to be a sound engineer, I do have long hair, and have spent a lot of time laying around. Work? Well, I guess I'm going to have to at some point! I spent 6 years writing computer software, then I went back to college to learn about the music business. Hobbies? The Special Programme of Initiative Challenge and Excitement. Basically an opportunity to do all those things you wouldn't get a chance to do otherwise. In my case this ranges from driving a tank to archery to inflatable Sumo wrestling.

Andy Brown was born in Mberengwa, a beautiful village that lies deep in a valley of the mountains of Zimbabwe. Almost every evening, as dusk surrendered to twinkling stars, the many members of his core and extended family would come together to sing, dance and drink away their fears of what the future held around the fire in traditional Karanga style. As 1986 dawned Andy merged his talents with ILANGA, which changed the course of Zimbabwean music with its fusion of Shona and Ndebele rhythmic styles, Zimbabwean traditional and Western musical sounds. Tunes of theirs such as "True Love" and "Silver and Gold" became overnight hits in the clubs and homes of the Zimbabwean people.

Andy Brown Software Consultancy was set up by Andy Brown in 1995 to specialize in the design of real-time software for electronic products. Andy has been involved with many of the hi-tech companies that have participated in the world famous Cambridge Phenomenon. Most of his experience has been with small, cost effective products for mass production. His maxim for embedded software is that *small and simple is beautiful*.

Andy Brown Wants You!

Master Gunnery Sergeant Andy is head of the Marine Recruiting Substation in Santa Barbara, California, where he's screened thousands of candidates to find the proud few whom comrades can count on in time of war. In nearly two decades as a recruiter, Brown, 45, has earned a reputation as the "best Marine recruiter on the planet."

If anyone has entrepreneurial tendencies, it's Andy Brown. He started making twig furniture in his family's garage in 1988 and moved the operation to a storefront in New Buffalo soon after. Thanks to Mary's presence in his life and business, things have really progressed. She says he's spontaneous and creative while she is structured and practical. If you wander into Hearthwoods on Whittaker Street, you'll see the results of their teamwork.

Andy Brown is a Vietnam Vet, he races cars, and he has his own business repairing air conditioners and heaters. Andy's entry into the Fresno folk music scene was accidental. Andy met Kenny Hall at Ron Tinkler's house. Shortly after, Andy spotted Kenny hitchhiking. He asked Kenny if he could learn to play the guitar. Kenny took out his fiddle and played "Tommy Don't Go." He told Andy to follow him and see if he could change chords. Andy followed him through the tune, and Kenny said, "You can play. I can tell right away."

Andy Brown has been ranked the No. 47 prospect in the Midwest by SuperPrep as well as being selected All-Region by the National Recruiting Advisor. He is considered the No. 54 prospect in the Midwest and No. 19 offensive lineman in the country by Prep Football.

Andy Brown, President of Midstates Supply Company, was awarded the rank of *nidan* (2nd degree black belt) in 1992. He was an accomplished rugby player while a student at Princeton and has been practicing *Shotokan* under Jon Beltram since 1981.

After graduating from ACU, Andy Brown was hired by Los Alamos to continue work on the PHENIX experiment at BNL. He worked on the muon tracking subsystem where the main task was to construct the world's largest cathode-strip drift chambers. This experiment is the largest of four experiments on the Relativistic Heavy Ion Collider (RHIC) accelerator ring designed to examine the existence and characteristics of the quark-gluon plasma.

Since 1989, Andy Brown, Senior Naturalist and licensed bander has been making the rounds of the county trails banding bluebird nestlings. In the 8 years Andy has been banding, he has banded 700 bluebirds, and of these 700 over 200 have been banded just this year. It is a bumper crop year for the bluebirds of Calvert County!

Andy Brown was born and raised in Newcastle-Upon-Tyne which is in the North East of England. He does not work down in a pit or in the shipyards and if he were to wear a hat it would be a top hat. His dog of choice is a whippet due to its glossy coat and its overwhelming availability in his area.

During his school years Andy Brown was a target for the bullies because he was fat.

Andy Brown is the Strategic Biodiversity Planner for Anglian Water, developing the company's biodiversity action plan and over-seeing the conservation work at its reserves and operational sites. He is the company's day to day contact for the Osprey project and he holds the purse strings.

In 1974 Andy Brown became the final National Hockey League goaltender to play without a facemask.

"A slab of my work from the early 80s was defined by its ability to succeed when read at 2AM to drunken students. Among the poetry community "second aeon" became an arbiter of taste and a place to be seen. The Americans loved what I did yet I was never once in my entire career as a publisher mentioned by any national newspaper.... Prolific in bursts. Then long stretches of silence. That's the way it is now. I need an early start and really have to avoid speaking to anyone. People do not understand this, even those close to me."

— Andy Brown

STEPHEN CAIN

A History Of Canada

for Bill Hutton & George Bowering

1. WOLFE & MONTCALM

It's okay Montcalm you're only bleeding. But so is Wolfe so it's just like playing Risk. There's an Indian squatting nearby for some reason in West's painting although neither is Canadian. You can see it when you visit Ottawa although that won't be the capital for another hundred years. No chess set for this battle is available, but you can use Revolutionary uniforms and most won't know the difference. From Louisbourg to the Beauport Shore it's seven years of interchangeable imperialism. They died because of the Plans of Abraham and Isaac won't be pointing his pecker at Uncle Sam at Queenston for another fifty years.

2. THE WAR OF 1812

It's one we won. It's cows versus cowboys and the Flames want to merely march across the border. Speaking of arson, we got to burn Buffalo and the fires haven't stopped since. Every night it's a five alarm at SUNY and Bernstein can't absorb Tecumseh's *techne*. Creeley, Duncan, and Spicer move onto the Western Front, but Bromige and Blaser are already talking with Tallman. Now it's up to TISH to tamper with Olson and lead the charge to Kootenay. The project is blackened before it can be mounted, but no matter what Mathews mitigates it's a stalemate. Still, it was important—without it we'd have no army, no autonomy, no chocolate.

3. THE 1837-38 REBELLIONS

They're marching from Montgomery's Tavern to the Horseshoe. They want a micro-brew that speaks for them, one that tastes great and that's less filling. They want bull-frogs to boast about their beer. They want the Bud girls to bind them and give them Head. [Enter bpNichol bearing a sign that reads: "Meanwhile!"] All the cool kids belong to the Shadow clique and the Habs have no place to call home. The Patriotes turn to the Sons of Freedom, but they all want to be in Paris, they want to call the Mona Lisa mom. Papineau is holding a press conference outside the Chateau Frontenac and crying: "Fly like a Frenchman, sing like Celine."

4. SIR JOHN A. MacDONALD

Johnny's drinking CC with Daniel Jones at Sneaky Dee's. After each shot John A. turns his head to puke on the sawdust floor. "That's what I think of your writing,"

MacDonald growls. "You're a coward and you won't stop writing poetry." Jones agrees and looks around the bar for someone he knows. MacDonald pulls at Jones' T-shirt: "I like you. You're a good man. I know you would rather have John A. drunk than E.K. Brown sober." Jones can't help but agree. The punk kids are all around them, and they all want to write haiku. "This country can't afford to mythologize two drunks. You've got to give it up." Jones agrees, and does.

5. THE LAST SPIKE

"Leaping lizards!" murmured Good Ole Ned Pratt, the pupils falling from his eyes. He's filled with oatmeal and nodding off by the faculty lounge fire. The spirit of Scott is at his ear muttering, "coolie, navvy, where's the Alberta beef?" Has it really been that long since he made Modernism moulder *a mari usque ad mare*? In the famous photo Frye's in the foreground, Davies has the highest hat, but Marshall's got his hand on the hammer. Lee and Godfrey can't wait for their turn to take a swing at the gold-plated university pen that bent at the first strike. Berton took the photo but Birney thought it was bullshit.

6. LOUIS RIEL

Riel never had a problem with back bacon. He ate MacDonald's hamburgers, drank Lake Michigan soda, and wore a pin with a crest that read "*Peau de Bison.*" The Metis rallied the frogs, fish, and ducks to their defence, but the lakes, creeks, and ponds were on crown land. Something happened at Fort What's-His-Name but Batoche's no Baton Rouge. Singing "Alouette," not "Lafayette," Riel asked Rudy to set the record straight. Bugger Big Bear, it wasn't about boundaries, it was all about the Governor General's rewards that Gabriel didn't garner. Riel wasn't hung for treason. He was executed for being a poet and D'Arcy McGee was jealous.

7. THE KING-BYNG AFFAIR

Nobody has confidence in the system anymore. M.T. Kelly is better than Ondaatje? MacLennan trumps Watson? Somebody has to speak for the people and overthrow the tyranny of the Governor General. At Grossman's the rabble is rising: who's fit to bestow the laurels, aren't people poets too? Naim Kattan asks Michener to absolve the disastrous 1969 results but this is unprecedented—haven't his decisions enshrined such luminaries as Gwethalyn Graham and Igor Gouzenko into the national consciousness since Bertram Brooker first took the crown? The poets drink at the tavern for four days; on the fifth day Milton emerges victorious.

8. THE OCTOBER CRISIS

Pierre Trudeau is cracking walnuts with a hammer. The FLQ want to smoke pipes but Fidel will only allow them cigars. The Canada-Cuba cabal is cancelled and Loyalists are asking for their land back. George Woodcock says remain calm. It's a crisis in CanLit before it's even been christened and Maggie's just published Susie's journals while singing Gloria Gaynor's song. Last year was the year of the spider and the acid freaks are stoning gloves. Why isn't Quebec happy? Their country is not a country, it's winter. And it comes too early, in October. They don't want a 'sea-change', they want the seasons to change.

9. PAUL HENDERSON & THE 1972 CANADA-SOVIET SERIES

Gord says she never gave a fuck about hockey and neither did I. The Oshawa Generals drafted a lot of date-rapists who billeted with local families. There's a Bobby Orr lounge at the Civic and Eric Lindros went Coo-Coo at Bananas. There's a movie called *Pray for Me, Paul Henderson* and now he's a born-again Christian. He kicked the Godless Soviets' asses and now he wants to do the same for Canada. Henderson never visited my school but Eddie Shack did. Eddie told us to stay in school and I've never left. There's an Eddie Shack Donuts down the street from Tim Horton's in Oshawa. You can smoke in one, but not the other.

10. TOM THOMSON

Tom's portrait of Emily Carr was the bridge from his early Impressionist work to "Les Demoiselles d'Orillia." She was sitting for her portrait in his Toronto studio and thinking about a book of small literary Cubism. She would go on to write anyone's autobiography. He was thinking about taking canoe lessons to improve his j-stroke. Two months later as the lake turned as murky as a Milne, as hard as a Harris, it looked like a barn was floating on the surface of the water. Anger was in his mind as the liquid filled his lungs: "Those fuckers will never get it right. There's no 'p' in my name. I was never one of the Seven."

IN CONFIDENCE

Acting out in secret,
Holding it in at the office,
Pretending I'm William Hazlitt,
Essayist of said orifice,
Receptionist with wit.

It's better than being jobless,
Considering I'm a postgraduate,
Making one's name with promptness,
And getting things done lickety-split.
I am immediate.

I keep my workspace spotless,
All my pencils seriate,
My drawer is a necropolis,
For the surplus of retrofit,
As if I give a shit.

No one knows I'm a poet,
Holding it in at the office,
Inside weaving tercets,
But outside willing to submit
Their lists in triplicate.

SPECIAL CASES (PREVIOUS OFFICE EXPERIENCE)

She, in the midst of all, preserved me still
A poet, made me seek beneath that name
My office upon earth, and nowhere else.

—William Wordsworth

Mrs. Bortman, my boss
at the Jewish Family Services Office
believed in me, and showed
me how to work the phones.

Within a week I knew
the locals of all my favourite
secret service officers,
I mean, social workers.

One sexy social worker
seemed so ditsy and sheltered
I was aroused thinking of her
in her office, in potential danger.

But most of the 'clients'
(never call them 'cases',
Mrs. Bortman taught me)
were just lonely and depressed.

Like me. They posed no threat
but unto themselves. Forsaken, and justifiably alone
some didn't care enough to bathe, while others
came dressed as if for a wedding.

One young Franco-New Brunswickian social worker sensed
my bittersweet personality and took me out for a beer.

He described in detail why he had been
circumcised at the age of thirty-five.

This was supposed to interest me
in his foreskin-less penis, but I just kept thinking
how painful it must have been for Abraham
to make his covenant with God so late in life.

TO UPPER MANAGEMENT, WITH GRATITUDE UPON MY RECENT VIVISECTION (FALSE MEMO III)

I accept your recent "suggestions and guidelines"
sparked, I presume, by the growing height

of my Hall's mentholyptus desk sculpture
(done exclusively on MY FREE TIME,

not YOUR TIME, as you insinuate),
and my "Famous Missionaries as Cuddly Kitties"

screen savers. I had no idea that some of my Jewish
co-workers find my cuddlies "appalling" (as you put it).

I accept your "helpful tips" and "things worth thinking about"
with laughter, though they cut me open like a cat.

I don't care what anyone says, Sir Henry Morton Stanley
as a fuzzy York Chocolate youngun' IS adorable,

And the cherished David Livingstone
as a Ragamuffin-Cheetah lad is adorable AND

prophetic: His body is buried in Westminster
Abbey, his heart interred in Zanzibar.

But I suppose I must try not to expect so much
from people. Things like courtesy and understanding.

Why don't you just pinch my pineal gland
and draw the juice up like a tear through a straw?

Why don't you just eat my fish meat,
you motherfuckers, and choke on my bones

like ivory paperclips, like a spine of
alabaster staples. Choke on them, and die.

It's not the Tower of Babel, you freaks,
it's the Taj Mahal. The Taj.

THE WIND DIVIDER

Träumend an der Schreibmaschin'
saß die kleine Josephin'...

—Gilbert and Profes

Hovered and swiveling behind the gray
cloth wall of her cubicle
divider, she makes me seek into my drawer
for more than pencils. My rebel
typewriter girl who goes to the movies
alone soaring to screen
on the paper-clippèd wings
of my lighter / darker imagination.
Green ice-flashes of the Photostat machine
ignite her as St. Theresa in passion. She glides
past my station in white stockings
and Wallabees, red ones, like some devil nurse
prepared to I.V. the water cooler
with one scarlet ink cartridge.
Her hair black and shiny as trash bags
overstretched in their receptacles, so well groomed,
the best kept secretary, with airs, inviolable,
like a sadistic Veronica working in an office
just to spite daddy. Or, my clean new American girl
as comfortable with Pitman as with Gregg,
tomboyish and undemanding, her fantasies
refillable, mine untold: (At the typewriter in a dream/
Sits my little Josephine... /my longing tapped
upon her keys/ but she'll require more keys than these...)
Spied through loose-leaf
reinforcements, I can smell fresh duotang,
taste the gluestick like sorrow on my lips,
hear the dust of rubber erasers
falling like little blackened frowns,
feel her like a pocket full of Parker Posey.

IVORY LETTER OPENER (FALSE AIRMAIL MEMO)

Well, the egos on these bozos,
won't fit into standard next-day
shipping boxes; are too heavy
to return to The Prick Zone.

Snug in its alligator holster,
waits my cool ivory blade,
until our head Marketeer de Sade
shows a desire to re-upholster.

Then with my ivory I'll be slashing
innocent and unsuspicious
envelopes and secret memos,
buckskin armchairs down to coil springs.

'Till then it's words make me feel free,
and bluish bruises, red incisions,
are the checkered border of my signed
and sealed air-mail displacency.

MARGARET CHRISTAKOS

M1. U.K. BREAST MILK TOXIC: 13 JULY 99

with each line prematurely weaned to escape charges of plagiarism

chemical cocktail   of pollutants
to higher   than of
toxic substances,   the babies
being exposed   limit daily
range of   from incinerators,
pesticides and   350 contaminants,
including some   and dioxin-like
tissue highly   lethal headlines
most recently   in animal
feed, introducing   food chain
including milk   was agent

Agent lethal recently was milk highly most including chain dioxin-like
introducing in food 350 limit and feed, daily exposed some
animal toxic being including headlines higher — and tissue chemical
— from contaminants, — — of pesticides — — the
incinerators, — — of range — — than babies —
— to substances, — — of pollutants — — —
cocktail

N1. Nice Boy

me! Don't

Eat me!!

now! Corrupt

Meee!!

N2. NICE SHEEP

little boy me! Don't
the cow Eat me!!
let's get now! Corrupt
where is Meee!!

he's under
fast asleep so beautiful.
hey, you me. Baby......
yes, you blanket on.

gimme some know where
come closer
let me a fucking
blue manhood fucking break!!

the making break!!! Shut
your heartbeat shut up!
down blow and shut
nice boy door and

in a fuck outta
nice boy outta here!!
the haystack here!!! Cop
blue boy a feel

looks after already!!!
the sheep

N3. NICE HORN

little boy — — cocktail the
cow of pollutants — let's get
substances, — — where is —
— to fast asleep babies he's

under hey, you — — than
yes, you — of range gimme
some the incinerators, — come closer
pesticides — — let me —

— of blue manhood — from
contaminants, the making and tissue chemical
your heartbeat headlines higher — down
a toxic being feel nice boy

exposed some animal in blanket and
feed, daily nice throbbing food 350
limit the haystack dioxin-like introducing in
blue boy most including chain looks

after was milk highly the sheep
agent lethal recently the corn loving
a hunk — come blow!!!

JON PAUL FIORENTINO

I Wanna Be Your Alpha Male

My parents sucked. They used to make me mow the lawn despite my lethal allergy to freshly-cut grass. On a weekly basis, they made me wear a surgical mask and start up the old gas engine mower and mow the fucking lawn. There I was, wearing a baby-blue surgical mask, pushing this obnoxiously loud machine over our lush green grass. As one might imagine, the neighbourhood kids were ruthless. They called me everything from Dr. Lawnmower, to sissy, to douchebag, to fuckface. Dr. Lawnmower. That sounded kind of cool—like a supervillain. When I was finished mowing the lawn, I had to empty the bag of grass clippings. My entire body was one huge blazing rash except for an oval shape patch of white skin on my face where the mask had been; and, because of my severe asthma, I generally had to take a triple-dose of inhaled steroids and ventolin to catch my breath. I am not bitter.

Once, when I was around 14, after emptying the grass-clippings into a bright orange garbage bag, I heard a taunt ringing in my ear: "Hey Dr. Lawnmower! You're stupid, you stupid lawn-mowing fuckface!" There was a group of around four boys on the street, much younger than me, pointing and laughing: "Dr. Lawnmower! Dr. Lawnmower! Fuckface! Douchebag!" I ripped my mask off and charged toward the kids like a raging, asthmatic bull. I inspired no fear. As I approached the clear leader of the taunting band, I began to swing my fists wildly. The combination of physical activity and allergenic activity resulted in a blackout before I could land one effeminate punch. I lay there, my body on the edge of the grass, my head on the curb. My parents told me later that when they arrived on the scene, the boys were laying the boots to me. I think my mom may have done a little stomping herself before calling the ambulance—that would have been just like her. Anyway, before my eyes opened in the St. Boniface Hospital emergency room to a fluorescence of antiseptic, anesthetized, swirling hospital-type stuff, I saw you for the first time. Bright orange hair, wild, untamed freckles, a gap between your two front teeth just like David Letterman. You were my dream girl—Anne of Green Gables without the Green Gables and much hotter, and willing do to really freaky things that Anne of Green Gables would never do unless she was paid a shitload of money and even then I'm not so sure she would do those things, but you would. Even as repeated injections of Prednazone were yanking me from my unconscious state, the vision of you remained clear. You were, and are with me.

My parents tried to convince me that I would never marry. They told me I was too fat and asthmatic for marriage. They told me that the most I could hope for was to be a general labourer who pays for sex on a monthly basis and has a disturbingly large collection of fetish pornography. They even had a nickname for me: "Future Blue-Collar Pervert." Actually, my parents had a few nicknames for me. My dad liked to refer to me as his "Big Wheezy Sweat Monkey" and mom preferred to call me "Captain Failure". General labourer, fetishist—I've achieved that life for myself now but I'm not satisfied. I know you are waiting for me somewhere.

Now that I'm all grown up and my parents are dead, I want a girl like you. In fact, I want you. A girl with taste and style and a house. I bet you have your very own house. I want to turn that house into a home. I want to have fat asthmatic babies with you. How much do you pay on your mortgage each month? $700? $800? I know I can afford my share. Let me win your bread. Let me pay some affable, pimple-faced kid with no allergies to mow our lawn. Let's watch him from the window; I will hold you close and we will watch him manicure our lush grass in perfectly symmetrical rows. You might have the heart to offer him lemonade or, if we are feeling perfectly subversive, a cold Coors light, or perhaps some homemade wine. Perhaps we can share a hobby of making homemade wine. The first attempts might be a little cloudy but we'll get the hang of it. With you by my side there would be nothing I couldn't do. Except maybe sit-ups. Those are really hard. Maybe I will videotape our lovemaking and we can go over it as if it was game film. (I will wear a surgical mask.) You can be my coach. No. I will be the coach. You will be my star player.

Hey. Listen. Screw that. I want to mow your lawn. Screw that hypothetical kid. He can get a hypothetical paper route. Let me mow your lawn. I wanna mow your lawn. It will be worth the rash, the hives, the lack of oxygen. I wanna mow your lawn. I wanna be your alpha male.

COREY FROST

A NOTE ABOUT THE AUTHOR'S NAME

The name of the author of this work is Corey Frost,[1] which is a real name and not a pseudonym. The results of an informal poll indicate that this is a good name for a writer. Let's examine the reasons why.

Frost, of course, is the name of the famous American poet, Robert Frost, who seriously contemplated suicide. His work is among the most accessible modern writing, given the central theme of all his collections: the quest of the solitary person to make sense of the world. Consultant in Poetry at the Library of Congress starting in 1958, four-time winner of the Pulitzer Prize, Frost is one of the most widely-known poets of the century in the United States: a true poet of the people. The name Frost, however, is relatively uncommon in America and perhaps as a result it has acquired vaguely aristocratic connotations. It has been suggested that this was a factor in Frost's popularity among the working classes. Robert Frost died in 1963. For obvious reasons, it would not be appropriate for a writer to have exactly the same name as such a famous poet—aside from problems of brand confusion and issues of copyright, the name might suffer from a taint of unoriginality. It is, however, effective to capitalize on the prestige of the poet's last name while updating it with the addition of a more contemporary first name.[2]

According to architect and theorist Charles Jencks, 1972 marks the end of modernism and the inauguration of the postmodern era. More precisely, the transition occurred at 3:32 pm, on July 15th of that year, when the Pruitt-Igoe housing development in St. Louis, Missouri, a modernist masterpiece, was dynamited because it was uninhabitable. Corey was a popular name for children born in 1972, which was the year of the author's birth and also the births of Corey Haim and Corey Feldman, who would go on to be teenage film stars of the nineteen-eighties. They would have strangely parallel careers. Corey Feldman was born first, in Reseda, California. Corey Haim was born soon afterwards in Ontario, Canada. Both began their acting careers around the age of eight, at the beginning of the eighties, both eventually winning acclaim in the middle of the decade, Feldman for his role as the easily-excitable Teddy Duchamp in *Stand by Me*, and Haim for the title role in *Lucas*. The story of how they first met, or what agent or producer first had the idea of getting them together, has not been widely documented, but in the late eighties they began to co-star in a number of films, including *The Lost Boys, Dream a Little Dream*, and *License to Drive*. Both Coreys seemed to embody the spirit of the eighties teenager, and appealed strongly to that group. However, with the transition to a new decade, and as they both entered their twenties, their appeal waned and their roles became less and less prestigious. Never quite attaining popularity with a wider demographic as did Michael J. Fox or River Phoenix, both Coreys were relegated to low-budget hack comedies, such as 1994's *National Lampoon's Last Resort*, in which they both appeared.

It is difficult to say whether Haim and Feldman's success in the eighties imbued the name Corey with a certain star quality, or whether it was in fact the contemporary currency of the name itself that made the Coreys seem more "cool" to eighties audiences. Corey Hart, a pop singer from Montreal, Quebec, who was also very popular in the mid-to-late eighties, seems to have contributed to or benefitted from the same phenomenon. In any case, the appeal of the name was definitely overspent and wore out quickly. Today the popularity of the name Corey is in decline. The nineties saw a massive decrease in enrollment for the fan clubs of teenage pop stars named Corey. Recent baby name books implore mothers to refrain from naming their sons Brett or Corey.[3] Why the sudden backlash against Corey?

The name Corey seems to connote an immodest optimism that is perhaps too characteristic of the eighties for the tastes of the more world-weary nineties and naughts. It is not a traditionally popular name, hence its appearance in the seventies when there was a growing acceptance of the arrival of societal change. (Note that in the fifties, movie star Corey Allen was not considered to have the star appeal necessary for a lead role, and was cast rather as the villain—for example as the antagonistic yet ultimately tragic Buzz in *Rebel Without a Cause*.[4]) Against the background of the neo-conservative eighties, it would have had the appeal of the safely unusual, along with other trendy names like Jordan, Kirk, Brent, or Alex, without the extravagance of earlier "hippy" names like Rain or Peace. The fact that these names were chosen for their originality by thousands of baby boomer parents at the same time is oppressive evidence of the deterministic omnipotence of demographics. The name Corey, then, is representative of the failure of creativity in the post-psychedelic, media-dominated society of the late twentieth-century, and that is why is it somehow repulsive, while at the same time fatalistically endowed with its own nostalgic kitsch value. Corey symbolizes a generation who were optimistically brought into and brought up in a materialistic world, only to find on reaching adulthood that the optimism had run out.

The author's middle initial is J. The queerness of this letter is exemplified by the fact that in Scrabble™ Brand Crossword Games, there is only one.

Notes

1. When I was eight years old, I begged my mother to buy me blue leotards. I'm versatile and easy-going, and I'm a quick learner.

2. Stress can lead to the dissipation of mental energies. A pseudonym is only as good as the paper it's written on.

3. If you want to sing out, sing out.

4. That's the edge. That's the end.

   Yeah. Certainly is.

   You know something, I like you. You know that?

   Why do we do this?

   You gotta do something. Dontcha?

   Crunch! Line 'em up.

   You OK?

   Yeah gimme some dirt.

   Judy? Me too.

   Mmm?

   Um. May I have some dirt, please?

   Hit your lights!

   Aaaahhh!

   Where's Buzz?

   Down there.

   Let's get outta here.

   Down there. Down there's Buzz!

   This is fine.

   You be all right?

   Judy? You wanna see a monkey?

   Hey, you wanna come home with me? I mean, there's nobody home at my house and heck I'm not tired. Are you? You see I don't have too many people I can talk to.

VALERIE JOY KALYNCHUK

PROJECTS POINTFARM

Amanda and Christina's brother Jason is 'sent away' for trying to set them on fire. I really like to play with them. They make really good pretend Oscar acceptance speeches.

Carrie only has a mum too. I play with her sometimes though she is two years younger than me. She is five and I am seven. One day, when asked what we should play, she suggests we "Pretend we're kissing Michael Jackson's penis." I know there is a reason I don't want to play this but I am not sure what that reason is. I go inside and watch television.

Rodney wanders the development with a lawn mower every day during the summer. Sometimes he actually cuts the grass. Mostly though, he just pushes the mower up and down the sidewalk, a beer always in one hand. This goes on for years. Rodney has a wife, but she is rarely seen. One year Rodney and his mower are no longer a fixture of my summer because he has apparently bled to death on his kitchen floor. My mum says his years of drinking booze ate a hole in his stomach and everything just poured out.

James is retarded. When he comes outside he lumbers through the development singing "Electric Avenue" and clapping his huge hands. The other kids regularly make him pull down his pants and laugh at him till he starts to cry. One day he gets his bell bottoms caught in his bike chain and everyone runs away. My mum is the only one who will help him get them out. I feel sorry for him all the time till another day when he goes berserk and pins me down in my back yard, straddles me, and scratches up my face. My screams get my brother's attention who turns the garden hose on James. He cries and runs off.

No one knows which unit little Mary lives in. She is about four, always outside, morning till after the street lights come on. She's dirtied and her hair is too matted for the good of a comb. She follows us around especially when we have food. We are outside Alanna's house with ample chocolate bars and Lik M Aid and little Mary is being too pushy for Alanna's liking and she grins. She will teach her a lesson. She goes inside for a few minutes and returns with a small aluminum plate filled with some sort of liquid. She offers it to little Mary who takes it eagerly and drinks it down, giggling furiously because all the other kids are. "What was that?" "It was pee!" I go home and watch television.

Jodie and Jason aren't allowed to come outside very much. Every time they do it isn't long before their dad appears from around the corner and tells them to "Get the hell home now!" One day they are brave and whine that they wanna stay outside and play. Their dad tells them they are "Fuckin' little brats and one day I'm gonna kill you guys and bury you in the back yard!" The kids follow him back, don't cry, not a word. I am worried but less so when I consider the back yard. With the six squares of cement and the tiny flower bed I can't see how there'd be room to bury dead bodies. Even very small ones.

The skin and bone Mennonite lady tries her best but her teenage daughters are so angry they move in with boyfriends and get pregnant. Her oldest boy has quit school and waxes his car high. Only one chance left in the last son, a junior high nerd, and me, the little blonde girl from across the street. We eat baloney on a bun and do Bible study or watch *Love Boat*. Christmas is cookies and angels made out of toilet paper rolls. Oh gosh I wanna be good so she'll say God thinks I'm good.

Number 14 is the only one bedroom unit. The old couple keep to themselves. We see them on the 11 bus. They don't sit together and never speak. I am confused when my mother tells me they are brother and sister cause there is only one bedroom. They always turn off the lights on Halloween so the kids won't trick or treat.

Alanna is mad at me, throws a shingle from the church parking lot. Black eye, have to tell. Alanna's mum shows up on our steps, firm grasp on her kid's arm. Demands she apologize to me and my mum, says don't worry she can control her kid, smacks her in the head, blood, screams, drags her home. By the hair. I shoulda lied said I just fell. Which is what I figure Alanna will do tomorrow at school to explain her eye.

The lady in number thirty-eight has to leave her little boy alone just for an hour or so. He turns on the stove, climbs up on the elements, and the rubber of his runners melts down and he can't get off. All kinds of things with sirens are there when she gets back. Very bad burns and he isn't ever going to look the same. I overhear that the-asshole-super has told her to "Get in there and clean that crap off, I'm not cleaning that!" I figure that means he wants to keep the stove for another unit. That seems scary and he's so mean and what if we are cooking with a stove in our unit that—

Everyone knows Cheryl's family moved here from another development after her little sister got killed by a drug addict who threw a brick at her head. Shayna knows for sure cause they used to go to the same school. But one day to be mean she innocently asks Cheryl, "Where's your sister?" I gasp but Cheryl just shrugs and says, "She got killed." Then she runs and does a perfect one-handed cartwheel. I glare at Shayna and yell at Cheryl, "Wow, you're so good. I can't even do a two-handed one!"

RYAN KAMSTRA

THRU FUTURE PARTIES THEN WE CAME

The moon came down
on two motorcycles in a giant mesh metal globe.
A warehouse of replicated rainforest.
Skimpy speedos, water wings.

Amid a party drug scene
an automaton, ecstatic, was crying.
In bathroom where the real party was
a DJ frowning, said
to paneled mirrors of his silver wig & drag
     lifting nose-ring from odiferous powder
     —This sex tease is on a quest!

     —Have we yet to have the city life
     that no one else has had?
     Foam water-slide bisexual orgies?
          Bodies, bodies, tight tight tops,
     a music for decarasouled ponies!

—Ephemeral as a cinema
lip gloss to lip gloss may touch
in stall & after laptop.
Be prepared to flush!

          —Crawl into the projection booth
          there stop the movies & the trance.
          Disaster, darling, disaster!
          If we cannot have the spectacle
          let us rearrange the dance!

Let us break the spine & throat
of everyone we desire most
passionate against porcelain wall.
Consume their members, names & numbers.

Remember their particulars
for we cannot hold on to all!

Collect their each little bit
in a little black box.
Each body tone, fluid, each scream.
Blend them into
one seminal fondue.
This world is a buffet & the gourmet is you!
A meat cream sauce topped by g-string!

He was on as mission
but could no longer see its face.
The death of the moon of visions sent him
pods of ambiguous monsters
through membranes of the dance cave.
Retro music, lost in space.

oNCE uPON a tIME, iN mAGICAL pOLICE wORLD

Once upon a time
in magical police world
soldiers wore golden chaps
in ass-slapping columns at the dance cave.
TV personalities made history.
Guns blew bubbles.

Everyone was famous
so human gods thought fit to judge
from a pulpit of public sofas.
Bombs of a cloudy authority
rained down on paradise.
Order restored
with premier endorsements
after plenty interesting talk.

In magical police world
hush baby—no one dies.
You & me've been missing in action
since stepping out of time.

The trenches are crowded
by our waitstaff. Our vacation is
complete. Opposing weekend warriors
trade piss at urinals
slip pills between one another's teeth.

Our tour of duty
is a magical mystery.
Everyone is guilty, quiet as Earth.
If you got shot on being born
then we'll paint in your after-birth.

We melt in a puddle
before each bubble gun
suck best for each sharp shooter.
Trade in affection
for a permanent erection
if available or
the dude with the blackest boots.

Down here we princesses
love security.

REAL TV, OR CREATION'S MISTRESS' LONGING FOR THIS WORLD MANIFESTS AS PROGRAMMING

The floods came.
She was in her living room
awaiting the mailman.
Chances on this island
were placed at one in ten.

She likes the TV
bachelor, distrusts
his money-grubbing suitors.
Wardrobe arranges them
like ancient slave girls
about his jacuzzi.

Then closing her eyes
for the mailman
invites him in for tea.
Peels the bachelor's semblance
from the televisual projection
wraps it around
his chest, his thigh, his mouth.

Via closed circuit monitor
from an upstairs office
her husband watches
while she fucks this
stranger frankly.
His apathy invokes in him
an almost open-mindedness
& besides, there is no hockey.

Lampman's "The Hedgehog"

There was no surrender when he sported wood,
plundered the ravine, while he stood
among willing greenhorns in rose red pumps,
O plunging the valleys, again the mountain's rump;
mercilessly plumbed with hairy curiosity,
with a puffy cuckholder's careless glee;
maidens primeval, by fields of goldenrod,
dreaming of heights on castle rock,
fall to the snipe-like charm of the woodcock
and sing your simple jeremiad to the hedgehog.

B- / C+

"This is a most interesting paper,
David, you have a rare sympathy
for both Osric and Arthur Carlson—
intriguingly placed in the middle
of your paper on W.H. Auden.
Auden undoubtedly read Shakespeare
(though that quote you employ on page 7,
'Billy drooped like potato plastica,'
should not be attributed to Auden,
or any poor poet, for that matter),
and maybe Auden had a take on Hamlet
that stretched to its scene-stealing fop,
but it is most likely he did not,
as you suggest on page 12,
'sympathize deeply with the quaint argot
of Les Nessman.' W.H. Auden
sadly died in 1973,
a full 5 glorious years before
WKRP in Cincinnati aired.
How would he have known Les from Jennifer?
Johnny Fever from John Caravella?
Besides the obvious anachronism
(and I'm not sure you're not just being droll)
there is a liveliness to your writing;
if not, as you say, 'academical,'
I was not bored into the arthritic grip
that usually accompanies my grading.
Maybe it's best to not impeach myself
reminding you the Spanish Civil War wasn't
fought over 'Iberian Stamp Taxing,'
and Medieval Denmark was not noted
for 'its painful shoes made from cockles.'
Not to harp on typos or grammar slips
or your penchant for calling the Moderns
'the prophets of *that's a pretty big if*,'
because, you remind me of a young me.

Just last month, I was high on vicodin,
(I mean, I was calling the TV 'Mommy';
I mean, I was hugging my shoes like children;
I mean, the disembodied head of Alf
floated in my kitchen saying, 'I love you
as much as I love the fancy mustards')
judging stories in a local contest—
all these homey tales of curious cats
and blowjobs on the side of a mountain.
I wasn't grossed out by the bad writing,
but, in a fog, appalled with myself:
I mean who am I to judge anything?
Was I any less naive when I set-up
my shelves in my little college office?
How I smiled like a fleet banjo player
even when 'well-meaning' colleagues assured
the season of my hiring was 'flukey.'
In their eyes I was just a bald barber,
funny around a comb, neighbourhood-loved.
As good as any nine-fingered butcher.
Laughed at, a palpable Herb Tarlek
mixing plaid with plaid in a swell of jeans.
Like Osric, I'm here to hang out in the halls,
to remind the departmental Hamlet
the King's wagered 'six Barbary horses';
like Arthur Carlson, to stammer assurance
that the station-format change to all rock,
Mother, is completely out of my hands.
So, David, I dream the same thing you do
and you know who I mean: she sits up front
and laughs when I bring up my theater days;
the humiliations of auditions,
learning obscure lessons while in full dress.
But, I'd never ask her to Mexico;
She'd assuredly miss her great home state—
the one with all the granite quarries—
the one where she pines for young men like you
who'll treat her poorly and get on their way.

So, don't wake up the Dean, little Arthur;
I bet you Uncle Ben had to listen
to endless stories about cooking rice,
probably sometimes wondered "how come
nobody ever asks me about potatoes?"
Is it any different for you, David?
Isn't your favorite episode predictable?
The one where live turkeys are dropped
from a helicopter? I bet anything:
my collection of ceramic ibises,
my copy of Stevens' *Harmonium*
annotated by a young Jim Varney,
my autographed picture of Susan Hawk.
A gleeless cog, a mere parking lot space,
I will not move. I can't give you an A
when you say Auden, to 'pay for a wig,
sold tremens-inducing diet pills to kids';
your comments may not lead to graduate school
but, David, you will always have a friend."

FROM ***LETTER(S) TO DEREK***

IVE BEEN TRYING TO KNOW WHAT IT IS TO BE,
                 tho the definition is always changing
          rhonda, telling me this morning
                  she had to write a paper

     on what it means to be human, what
                 does it mean, i askt?
                            it means
              wanting to know

what it means to be human. captain kirk
     was right,
            i said.

FORMER BEATLE IN LOVE (PAUL McCARTNEY)

little things that cant be repeated: what.

adapting to the new movement, as captain kirk said,
what keeps the human race.

hibernation is preferred to death.

shut down, like sleep (what doesn't kill),
& even brain cells grow slow back

RANDY SAVAGE'S MOUSTACHE

I had a dream that I was Randy Macho Man Savage and I tore my father's moustache off because at the time when I dreamt that I was in fact Randy Savage, I was unable to grow facial hair. Today this is only sometimes the case. I wore hockey tape around my knuckles, wrists and fingers. I strained my voice to talk in his desert sand tonsil strain. I was living the emulative dream, one that seemed like the natural progression from GI JOE and Star Wars. I mean, I knew I was never going to achieve Chewbacca, not without some serious drugs.

It wasn't so much a dream but an early 1990s adolescent ambition, as I knew I was not going to be a part of any real team dynamic. I was bored in school, and an arm-chair narcissist, self-defeating narcissist; it was a great idea to choose a wrestler who usually was the victim of some gang-up or mismanagement. As I felt about my own place in life, my best years were behind me. I only assumed Randy felt the same way; he was just doing a job now, and his clothing was becoming louder as each match dragged on.

For years I felt akin to Macho Madness, and would tan myself in April in the cold nipple backyards of East York, a Greek neighbourhood in Toronto with plenty of nipples and areas for tanning. It seemed I wanted that Sarasota tan. It seemed I got reverse frostbite, resulting in a blister on my lip and a welt shadow in red and pink along my rib cage and spinal column. I was ready however, to ring the bell. Or for someone to ring the bell. A church bell, a recess bell, a tool-sharpening bell, any sort of bell, even a bicycle bell. In an interview Savage said, "My dad was my hero. I saw a lot of wrestling growing up. I loved it as a kid and I love it now."

I had seen Randy Savage at Maple Leaf Gardens, twice, and at Wrestlemania VI in the Skydome, one of a dozen undercard matches to the Warrior-Hogan main event. Definitely a low point in both of our careers. As a closet fan of his, I felt particularly bad for him at Skydome. It was a low point in his life when he teamed with Sensational Sheri in a mixed tag team match against Dusti Rhodes and some hooker. He went by the name of Macho King. It was lame, but I hoped for the best. A few years later, around 1993 I suppose, my father and I had been booked for a few matches. My father was not an athlete; he collected coins and drank buckets of coffee, which wasn't actually coffee but liquid he saved from his midnight shift at the embalming academy. It was an unfortunate truth my little sister and I had to witness, my father crawled up on the couch, his dark wings or tails as he called them, asleep on his body, a chilly earth-sprinkling of clothing, waiting for the call, when the corpse was still warm, and he'd get in the black car in the driveway, after muttering to his company pager, I'm coming death, I'm coming... He was the Undertaker.

There are a whole lot of funeral homes in East York, and a lot of cemeteries as well. I would suggest twenty-three more tombstones than wrestling fans, but nonetheless, our gimmicks, our paths were chosen. I was more of a traditional performer, whereas my father was one of those wrestlers who had a job. In an interesting twist of fate many of the viewers wouldn't recall because they weren't there, I was at Maple Leaf Gardens, in early 1993, just before Bret Hart fought Yokozuna in an impromptu non-title match after Bam Bam Bigelow cancelled, or likely couldn't get across the border from his home in New Jersey and anyway there was a moment of silence for André The Giant. He had died of a heart attack a few days earlier. It was sad. I thought of his giant body, and his hands, how they were bigger than the heads of my sister and mine combined together with an additional head of lettuce, perhaps Boston, not Romain.

Savage, whose real name is Randy Poffo (yes, brother of the first poet of pro wrestling's poet laureate, Leapin' Lanny Poffo) and although he never made it to the big leagues, he had stints as a catcher with the minor league systems of the St. Louis Cardinals, Cincinnati Reds and Chicago White Sox for five years. However, since I was too small and couldn't afford league equipment for virtually every sport offered to me, wrestling was my calling. Like my sense of self, it was imaginary, and like my friends, it would never let me down. Because they too were imaginary. I figured, unless my friends were going to make plastic toys of themselves then I couldn't play with them. I was a lonely boy who believed the only way to succeed was to get a clean pin over my father and for the mayor or at least his dog to witness the event. This would, in my mind set everything right.

So we worked out a few angles but none of them really concrete. The age difference, it just didn't seem plausible that a 40-something would have anything in common with a 15-year old, so why would any fan believe they could pull off a decent match? It was very frustrating, but I persisted with management, even hand-sewing napkins specifically designed for the funereal barbecues so that there would be enough cloth to capture all the grease and varying condiments, and so that those who were beginning to follow my Uncle's path of toasted animal burial had a proper transportation system that would not offend the chef. The napkins were a heavy cloth, similar to a priest's robe; actually that is where I got the material. They were monogrammed with the letters BB. Beef burial. Looking back, I felt bad for my father, but he had a long time to learn how to cook, a lot longer than I had to learn how to monogram priest cloth.

One can scruff their brown and vomit endlessly in supremacy of taste, but for me wrestling was the adoption centre I never had. For it was always there, in a capacity all too visceral.

I remember reading by candle light while eating my third taco with my little sister, an article in *Macleans* magazine about pro wrestling. It was called "The Hard Sell." Men with muscles and moustaches begged me to stand up for myself. I knew what I had to do. I finished my taco and waited for my father on his favourite beeper couch. My father who, for what it's worth, couldn't act his way out of a Styrofoam finger, was no wrestler, and thus made my 'heel' character all the more vicious, especially when the police arrived. He would say to my Uncle and I, "He comes at me with Kung-Fu, I have to protect my family." Mainly I wanted him to get some exercise.

"When the police came, they threatened to take away his wrestling cape, that was a low point in his career," my sister said on a videotaped interview. "We'll have to distort her, she hasn't signed the release," my lawyer recently told me over pimento loaf and lime soup. These things are really personal. It's a power to the system of dreams and goals, aspirations if you will, that when we are determined as human beings, no one thing will stand in our way. That physical reality will bow and break at the whims of unabashed intestinal fortitude. Gorilla Monsoon told me that, or was it Jesse 'The Body' Ventura? *Intestinal fortitude*. I think I used that in an grade eight essay one time. My father and I had agreed to work sawdust into the match at some point, because of its thematic integrity. It seemed that we had a lot of heat between us about the state of his workshop, and apparently this would come across in the match and those doing colour commentary would be able to refer to the sawdust with a bitter tone. *"You know how much that workshop means to him, this is really personal folks."* Something like that.

Recently with my lawyer I revisited these glory days of domestic wrestling through these Super-8 movies taken in my childhood backyard. I know it sounds a bit too convenient having a lawyer throughout one's childhood with a Super-8 camera to record everyday happenings, but I swear it's proved invaluable to me. Meat everywhere, the sizzle of barbecue and the girth of cotton ingratitude fortified the pasty colours that, over the years have waned, as if dropping from the moment in which they were captured. Ungrateful butterflies we all were, getting fat and tanned in the backyard, thick mayonnaise souring with bee spit. Yuck, what a gross nightmare. What kind of athletic career could I have hoped for eating the crappiest wonder bread last suppers like that? Suddenly I see the screen flicker yellow and its my dad cooking what was once some sort of pet, I think my sister and I may have even named her, what the fuck, so I was watching these films the other day with my lawyer, and my father looks like he's pregnant. "I was trying to film him from the stomach up," he said to me, and I looked at him, unable to finish my club sandwich, which by this time had curled into a shriveled eye monocle. I put it in my eye and watched the rest of the film. I was amazed at how my father's stomach under the tight and obviously sweatfucked t-shirt appeared to be eclipsing the backyard. The food was burnt that was for sure. My Uncle always complained to me in secret about my father's cooking, and would often take me back deep into our backyard and made me bring a shovel while he pantomimed consumption and ask me to dig a deep hole, where I was instructed to carefully hide the barbecue corpse and to "never speak of this again." Of course I told my sisters and the Randy Savage fan club roster. But to humour him I agreed, this was our secret, and I knew that my Uncle, all 110 pounds of him was not really disgusted with my father's cooking, and just being fussy, but rather was simply a fucking anorexic psycho. So I would constantly attack my father in my Dracula cap, only I reversed it so the red was on the outside and I would tell him that I was going to bodyslam him one day. I threw him through our coffee table, and it wasn't like the times on TV when they go through the table. This just sort of knocked out my dad because it was oak.

One time in the driveway we had a garden tool match and he cut my arm with a weed pick. Then he broke down my door while I was filming an interview and strangled me. It was great footage! My father later confessed to a small newspaper (or he had scrawled it on a napkin and photocopied it over a newspaper) that he had secretly been studying aggressive gardening videos from the library to counteract my adolescent rage. I of course upped the ante by working out regularly, and taking my version of steroids, expired Flintstone Vitamins. Also, to encourage rage, I would find packs of cigarettes that were not his brand, and line the kitchen floor with them and lead them out the door and into the backyard, ceremoniously near the unmarked grave of dead hotdogs my Uncle had stationed earlier in the story. I had to buy time for the main event, which was happening under sprinkler ejaculation later in the Spring. I kept extending the cigarette trail three miles at a time until he eventually ended up spending a weekend in Scarborough tracking down an elusive carton.

Meanwhile back at home I had both the gardening films and the WWF to keep me in shape.

Luckily my lawyer wasn't filming, because the footage would have created this rift within the family dynamic, and picnics and Chinese Buffets and my Uncle's talks on hot dog excavation nights would have been compromised. In retrospect, my father and I wrestled in what the business calls 'dark matches' that is, matches that an audience sees, but are not televised, nor are they part of a storyline. So in fact, my relationship in the ring with my father and his yellow gut was all in vain. But I still have the cape, the restraining order, and the garden tool, which I've melted down and wear as a therapeutic knee brace. Those were the dark matches where I learned the shape of my hands and elbows, the crook of the iron rails of our veranda, and the amount of give the fender of our car would give as I ascended into the air for a double ax-hammer. Those sweet afternoons, licking the sprinkler wounds of green and red stains into my near-copper knees.

EVA MORAN

I TEND TO THE TAIL END

The girls I work with over the summer in The Bay's Ladies Accessories Department decide that they want to have a "wild" night. They think it's a good idea to take me with them.

I know I am headed for trouble. One of these blonde, casual-wear, nubile braindeads is my floor manager. I like her. She's nice, in her context.

When we're at the swank club, I know the bartender. I fucked his roommate and later the same night, him. He sends free drinks our way.

The girls I am with finally catch the attention of some oversized, jock-frat-Bay street boys and, hell, I know I am in for a hard time picking up.

My floor manager swings her long blonde hair over her back revealing her Wonderbra breasts. I. I introduce myself as Eugene. I can't compete with blonde and breasts without the quirk.

Blondey smiles and flirts. I puke on Jare's shoes and drag him to the door by his tie, screaming, "What? Don't you wanna have a good time?"

Work. Big Boss Blond calls me into the office. *Fuck! Fuck! Fuck!*

"You're cray-zeee!" she squeals, and it hurts my fucking head but at least I still have a job.

She smiles, and asks me how my night with Jare went. I defer.

"How was your night with ah… guy?"

"When we went home, he told me he loved me."

Maybe it's that I'm hung, or maybe it's that she seemed to like me all "cray-zeee"-like, but, whatever, I decide to tell her the truth.

"Jare bent me over my kitchen sink and asked if he could ass fuck me."

Blondey stares blankly. I'm in for it. I've crossed the goddamn line. I rewrite my resumé in my head.

She's staring, earnest, saying nothing, and then...

"I wish someone would say they wanted to ass fuck me."

Jesus Christ! My world is exploding. I have a thought deeper than I've ever had. I have an Epiphany.

Gay men and porno whores have hoarded all ass action. And sure, I may seem biased because I belong to the latter category; I love to suck cock and have a landing strip groomed into my bald eagle snatch, but Blondey's words kick me in the kiester and I see the light:

EVERYBODY LOVES THE ASS FUCKING!

*

Lessons:

One: 1992. Scott Yang

The first time I let a hot rod ride up my homo zone,
I was a born again virgin. I wanted sex, but I didn't
want it to count. Ass fucking seemed like the only
solution to keeping me pure.

I went to the washroom after it was all over. When
I stood up to flush the toilet, I made a crucial mistake.
"Don't look down" is a rule that applies well to heights
and to an ass virgins' first trips to the washroom post-fuck.
Before my hand could hit the silver release handle on

the tank, the view in the bowl made me pass-out
and I rapped my head off the porcelain.

Scott Yang was bopping up and down playing guitar
when I finally came-to. Before helping me off the floor,
he put away his guitar and shoved modeling pictures
of himself in my face. He was having
a blast.

I asked him to take me home.

Fuck The Asshole. Do Not Be The Asshole.

Two: 2002. The second time. Richard Riley.

I got around to desiring the sweet meat between my cheeks
again in the first year of my MA. What can I say? My
mind frame was akin to that of the giggly Porky movies'
sorority girls in pink teddies or hot pants and nipple
popper tank tops; I was just waiting for the right man to
show me the ropes of a new fucktastic experience. Being
a near novice to the whole thing, there were physical
effects I did not expect.

Richard and I were taking a shower, and I felt like
exploring my newly ravished anus. My hole was goddamn
huge! I screamed at Rich, "Holy shit, dude! I could shove
a Nalgene bottle up my ass."

I panicked. I thought my asshole would never return to its
formerly pursed perfection. What did it mean to have a
constantly open orifice? Would I be able to hold in my
farts? Did I need Depends?

Do Not Panic. Things Return To Normal.

Three: 2002. Warren Klaus.

When Warren and I were driving to Halifax, he turned
his attention from the road to me. We were sharing
one of those road-trip moments of regretful honesty.

He told me that while masturbating he had once taken an
English cucumber up the ass. It really got him off. I was
baffled that anyone could get that many inches of food *up*
his shit shaft.

Later, when Warren bought me a bright pink vibrator, I
couldn't resist the urge to make him hurt so good. I got
him to beat-off while I massaged his insides with my
fuchsia cock engine.

Warren bought a John Cougar Mellancamp CD the
following morning.

**Straight Men Like Things Up Their Asses. It Is Fun For Everyone To Put
Things Up Ass.**

*

Last night, my epileptic lover turned over to spoon me and said, "I think it'd be really cool to fuck me while I was *grand mal*ing. I'd be all tense and jerky and shit. It'd be
a fucking ride, baby."

This from a guy who won't let me stick a finger up his ass while I'm giving him a
blowjob.

HAL NIEDZVIECKI

PUNK ROCK ROLE MODEL

Being alive means doing something you can never take back.

Bangs says to me: Do you know who I am?

I shrug.

I'm nobody, he says.

Me too, I say.

He gives me a broom. Sweep, he says. Cigarette butts, ash, dust pushed over a piece of cardboard. I take it outside, throw it at the street. He exhales a thick cloud, crushes a smoke under his boot.

You want the goddamn job?

I shrug.

Then shut the fuck up, he says.

He limps into the back room. Slams the door.

This is isn't his story.

I sell cheap electric guitars to factory workers and zitty high school rock and rollers. Made in Taiwan, that kind of shit, you put a Fender sticker over it, tell em it's the low end of a high class company. Cherry red, cut like a lighting bolt, real tight pants stuff.

It's not busy, and there's no actual mention of paying me.

I take half of everything, and sleep behind the counter.

That's what it's like on the payroll of a legend.

Not that he ever breaks down and tells me stories of the bad old days. With us it's strictly business:

That you making a fucking racket?

They gotta play 'em for me to sell them.

Keep it fucking down. Goddamn it. Can't even fucking hear myself think.

What's he got to think about? Takes two aspirins an hour, smokes pot like a baby sucking tit. The kind of pain nothing dulls. A chronic distaste for his life. A Dixs reunion out of the question, I guess.

Not that I give a shit.

Cheap fuck.

At night, I work a battered acoustic, tease it, animals whining, licking their wounds. I play slow and quiet, crooning from my stomach.

I'm waiting for him to trust me, because guys like that always end up trusting someone.

I close my eyes.

Sheils is fish net stockings, shiny long legs sticking out of a ripped Catholic school girl skirt that barely covers her ass. She has pink hair and gives great head. We moved in together, set up shop in a low-rise stinking of cabbage and curry. I was hungry all the time. We had a tv and a mattress. Sheils went to school and stole money from daddy. I stayed home and watched Happy Days. We watched TV all the time. Even when she was sucking me off, I was thinking about Joannie and Marion. Don't get me wrong. She loves it. It turns her on.

Best year of my life.

I hate fucking music, all that goddamn noise, who needs that shit? We don't ever listen to music.

I told Sheils: I want to live it, you know, I want to be there, living it.

That's what she loves about me.

One night, we drank Mad Dog, broke the bottle and cut our wrists. It was like a pact.

I wake up alone, the shop all street light shadows. I hear someone coughing and it's terrible, not like a dream, but the kind of instant that takes over everything and leaves your whole day foggy and diseased.

A pact's a pact though, and I won't let her forget.

As far as I can tell, Bangs has been reduced to a diet of white bread, soft cheese and yogurt. That explains the sour smell, like a used condom under a couch. I so much as mention it and he rips my weasely head off.

Fuck you, kid.

What does he want from me?

Comes downstairs a couple of hours later, eyes all glassy. How many aspirins can a guy take in one day?

When he was something it was a long fucking time ago.

Says: Good for the bones. Getting old, you know. He coughs this weird laugh, spits a wad of thick cheesy pale phlegm on the counter, looks at me.

He's dying, I guess. I mean, whatever, but Jesus.

Can you live on just cheese? Why should I care.

How do you live the big life? How do you open your arms and take it all with you?

I want to tell Bangs about my woman, about the scar on my wrist.

Late at night I put a paper bag on my face, sniff too much glue. It's like being really alive except you're not, except you're dead. I spasm and puke, out of control. I'm thinking: this is it, this is it, and I can feel the layers of skin peeling off, reality, you know. My eyes bursting like light bulbs. I knock over a stand of cheap ukuleles from Poland. They're made outta balsa wood. My head going crazy on the floor, firecrackers off my skull. And then it all becomes obvious. Because if you can hold on to the floor and get it all to stop spinning that has to matter, something has to matter, you choose, you know, you make your choice, but you stick with it.

He comes down wearing nothing but a pair of cowboy boots. He limps over to where I'm lying on the ground humping on the floor and he kicks me as hard as he can which really isn't that hard.

Next thing I know I'm crying, blubbering, and he's pressing my pukey face to his skin tight chest, just holding me, not saying anything.

Eventually, I start hearing this horrible music rasping against my ear drum, like a derailed train, the conductor on his way to the world to come.

He's singing to me. Jesus Christ, he's singing.

I barf on his balls.

I'll tell you what happened to us.

Before it was great. It was:

You wanna—

Yeah—

Oh baby, oh man, oh man, that's good.

Mmmm—

Joannie loves Cachie, you know what I mean?

I shouldn't have done what I did. Or else she had it coming.

It was that fucking brother of hers, real yuppie prick, in law school, if you can believe, gonna be a lawyer just like daddy. So the brother gets himself in a car accident, one too many highballs after court, sucks to be him. Ends up paralysed from the neck down. Sheils starts putting on outfits and heading for the hospital. Comes back crying every night.

How is it different? She hated him. Is it any different? I can just hear them taking her aside, whispering: come home, dear, your old room's just like you left it. It's like Fonzie's got a new girlfriend and Richie's fucking jealous.

She gets in, takes one look at me, runs into the shitter, locks the door. After a while, she comes out, sits on the mattress, starts crying again.

He keeps talking about killing himself, she blubbers.

Oh, yeah? Well he can't anyway. So forget about it.

I put my arm around. I slide a hand up her shirt. She pulls away.

I figure there are things you do and there are things you do if you have the balls to do them, if you know what I mean.

And then, before you know it, the super is up here looking for the rent she's supposed to pay.

Punk rock's a feeling. It's like a paper cut. You narrow down the wound to something so thick and deep you can't even feel it.

I don't know how to play the guitar. But I'm learning.

He was a hero. The skinny dying little prick.

I hike through backyards as long and smooth as golf courses. Maybe they are golf courses. Fall setting in, how long's it been since I've seen her? I'm thin and useless. I'm nothing. I'm nobody. Isn't that the way I wanted it to be? I've got my Dixs t-shirt on. Not much good when it gets dark and you can feel the wind on your nips and a dog starts barking at you when you light a joint in a gazebo—a gazebo!—so you bark back and then you think you hear sirens somewhere down the road and you get the fuck out of there.

We all have something to hide. Does it really matter? That's the million dollar punk rock question.

Running across front lawns, I can feel everything. I can feel the stiff grass pushing up through what's left of the soles of my shoes. I can feel perfect blades crushed under the bottoms of my feet, pins and needles, remember that Sheils? I wrote a song for her, just came to me one day, a different time, a different place, song like that could have taken us both all the way, you know what I mean?

needles and pins
needles and pins
they stick them in
pins and needles
c'mon kids
momma's hiding under the bed
hiding from your old school friends.

Kinda shit that doesn't mean anything, really, except that we all know exactly what it means, don't we? Sheils loves it.

Squirrels stopping to watch me.

I'll never be back.

I'll be back.

When it all started happening the kids were ciphers, a stack of blank fucking slates. You could write on us, our eyes were empty and when the music played you could see it slowly filling us up until the whites of our eyeballs were the colours of rage.

I mean, he hasn't exactly spelled it out or anything, but after a while you get to know someone even if they don't want to be known. You can't get anymore broken down.

Call Sheils again, her waspy little mother answers. Bet she wishes it was me filling nappies in a wheel chair. Bitch. I breathe heavy like a cripple trapped in a cross walk. 'Do not walk' flashing, you know what I mean? She hangs up.

The man's a mad genius. They never knew him, they never saw right through his stretched skin.

And the emptiness there.

He's lying on his back, white sheet, huge window, sun hitting, cutting strips into his pallid flesh. I put a hand over his mouth. He's still sorta breathing. Get him into a sitting position, fix him up with some glue. The bag over his face. He coughs once then he can't stop coughing. His whole body shaking, Jesus Christ, I've killed him, I've killed a legend.

Then he says: if you let the cat out, I'll cut your throat.

Cat? I say.

He's too weak to cut.

Quite a place you got here, I say.

All at once he pisses himself.

Fuck, he says. A pink rash seeps up his cheeks.

Girl comes in, starts wailing on a Yamaha. She's screaming and cutting up the strings with her long pink nails.

You're pretty good, I say.

She ignores me.

This as loud as it gets? she says.

She reminds me of Sheils: fresh-faced privilege, tartan skirts, attitude.

Fifty percent off if you blow me, I say.

You're disgusting, she says. You're a disgusting old man.

I turn up the amp, think of Bangs lying upstairs. I suppose I should call a doctor. Or, at least, I should have a week ago.

His ears buzzing old concerts, bleeding cracked lips muttering ripped off chords, hackneyed lyrics about dead cat guts and the fascist state. How many more aspirins? How many more joints?

Girlie rocks out, gets really into it. I can't hear anything.

Please, I beg.

I put my head between her breasts.

Feed him yogurt, smoke him up. Lean in to wipe his cheesy face. He grabs me in a head-lock, pathetic—I'm thinking, c'mon you old fart, you can do better than that.

You'll have to do better than that.

He says: who I am?

Who is he?

I have his heart, he has a heart that beats like it matters.

What the fuck, I say.

So this is the thanks I get.

I use his last five bucks to buy a bottle of sherry. Was even gonna let him have some, pour little capfulls into his mouth.

But surprise surprise, he's managed to drag himself down the stairs.

What the fuck did you do, he says, you cheap shit mother fucker. You little cock sucking mother fucker.

You should be dead by now, I point out.

He takes the pistol off his lap, wavers it in my direction.

I'm taking you with me, he says.

Today, tomorrow, what's the difference. Sheils, I think I'm coming for ya. I want the whole story. This is my story. I want to be really alive, even if it's just for a second. I'm thinking about a song. A song so pure nothing can touch it.

If this is living, then nothing can touch it.

After, I'll look back and see just a blinding flash of smoke, an amplifier on fire, and one way or another the dream will keep coming true.

Stay yourself, I yell. Don't ever change.

It's a few hours later but it feels like minutes, it feels like I've never left. I'm suppressing the urge to break the windows of luxury four wheel drive recreational vehicles imported from the continent to ferry gaz-guzzling idiots to and from the Price Club.

The old world is dead. Read it in the papers.

I content myself to throwing my empty bottle down the road where it skitters into the ink blot patches of darkness between ornate street lamps. Doesn't even break. That's 'cause it's snowing, it's starting to snow. I'm freezing to death, be the best thing for everyone. I imagine it this way, then that way. Bangs with a gun. Makes you sad, the way things have to turn out. I hold my hand up. I'm not surprised to see right through.

So this is it. This is being alive.

Bangs burns a hole in his head, lingers a little with the bullet lodged in his soft punk rock role model brain.

I get to the house, let myself in through the newly added cripple door. Nice and spacious. Very convenient.

Feel my way into the brother's room.

He's just in his bed, inert, impossible. I think of a record spinning, everything going in circles.

Then I hit the lights.

Who is it? he whimpers.

His voice is weak, like words, like history.

Get away from me, he says.

Sheils, I yell. Do you know who I am?

For her, I play a ferocious guitar.

Goes like this.

OTHER PEOPLE'S SHOWERS OR: "NO SOAP, RADIO"

With a cigarette hooked in the corner of his mouth, Perry waited outside the Kentucky Fried Chicken's front door. The cool, still November air and passive grey sky combined to create a pleasant contrast to the hustle and bustle of the inside—a welcome reprieve from the heat of twelve oil fryers working in unison, the dull, biting glare of yellow food lamps, and the pandemonium of beeping timers and ringing cash registers.

In his mind's eye, Perry could see a long beige station wagon with pseudo-wood paneling barreling down Labelle Boulevard, his girlfriend Tanya at the wheel. She flew past the mall, past the Speedy Muffler, and slowed for a red light beside Mike's Submarines. Perry imagined how she looked comically out of place—a nineteen-going-on-twenty year old speeding innocently through indiscriminate lane changes in the quintessential family car from another decade while the Indigo Girls sang out through an open window.

Then Perry's mind showed him a sweaty, dandruff-infested, mustached man behind the wheel of a light blue hatchback. The man's jeans were so tight he had to leave the top button open in order to breathe comfortably. Perry imagined the man angry, angry because Tanya's station wagon had cut off his car as they both passed the Telicino video store. He sped up to keep pace with the offending driver, eyeing the approaching red traffic light as an opportunity to articulate his disfavour with a symbolic hand gesture. Trying to choose between a shake of the fist and a raised middle finger, the hot and bothered man screeched to a stop alongside the station wagon. He looked across but felt his throat buckle. His right hand, readied for a muted expression of angry emotion, fell limp into his lap, useless and numb.

Perry created a glimpse of the future for himself, when the man, at home and alone, would throw himself on the floor, initiating a contained blizzard of dandruff in his living room, and weep.

Tanya sat patiently at the light, unaware of her annoying driving habits. Perry could see her milky skin, soft and young, clinging supply to raised cheekbones beneath brightly blinking green eyes. She reached to scratch her slightly upturned nose in a way that showed she had little concern for, or was even aware of, the possibility of onlookers confusing her itch for a pick. Tanya's hair, shoulder-length and coloured like a field of dying wheat, had been whipped about by the wind, and two thin strands were held inside the moisture of the corner of her mouth.

Perry's eye on the future saw the sweaty man wailing like an animal and pounding his living room floor with his fists, haunted by the memory of small red lips, pursing and unpursing in an unconscious attempt to free captured hairs. Perry could see how the sweaty man saw Tanya's lips. The man will never flip off another driver. He will never again take that risk. He will avoid at all costs the cold and biting nausea that went along with the slightest consideration of rendering insult upon the face of innocence, the face of beauty. Perry imagined his girlfriend's lips again, and smiled.

Perry could see all of this, past-present-future, despite the fact that he was at least a kilometre away from the cars, and at least an hour away from the mustached man's emotional breakdown. He wore a light autumn jacket over his Kentucky Fried Chicken uniform and held his paper hat in one hand. The outfit had a different feel to it out there, outside the restaurant at the end of a shift. The uniform didn't carry the same weight of pressure and responsibility that it did for Perry when he was inside, his hands caked with white flour while the oily stench of chicken and fries dripped from the walls and from his brow. The only weight Perry could feel now was the laggardly pleasant flow of nicotine rolling in his lungs and in his head. The cigarettes that came after work were decidedly different from the ones Perry smoked at other times. It was not the physical properties of the cigarettes themselves—he did not change brands to attain different tar levels, he did not switch from filtered to plain, and, despite an affection for the occasional menthol, he didn't save the minty greens for this special time. It was, however, the temporary feeling of autonomy that Perry felt in the first few minutes at the end of a working day that changed smoking. In those moments, while he could still feel that he was at the end of a shift and had not yet begun to think about the next one beginning, all of Perry's other responsibilities paled and faded because it felt so damned good just to not be at work. The air was cleaner, the sun more charitable, and the nicotine buzz was slightly more intense.

It was here outside, away from work, that Perry could think about where other people were and what they were doing in places where he could not actually see them. He imagined Tanya, on her way to pick him up. He imagined his younger brother, Greg, at home watching Saturday afternoon wrestling. He imagined a Japanese autoworker named Tom Yoritomo on the other side of the world asleep in his bed. Seeing people in his head that he didn't personally know was a lot more interesting than thinking about his friends and family. Perry could see himself standing and smoking on the solid soil of the North Eastern portion of the continent and feel others sharing the same landmass thousands of kilometres away. He saw the fields, the cities, the plains, and the mountains as his mind traveled West to visit a sales clerk tending to customers in a downtown Vancouver Gap franchise. Even more thrilling was the vastness of ocean to the East of him that led to a McDonald's maintenance employee, diligently painting the walls of a stock room in Frankfurt. "I wonder if it's true that they serve beer in German McDonald's," Perry mused.

Deep down, when watching a retired insurance broker chopping a cord of wood in the white snow-capped mountains of Wyoming, or a sweaty man with a dandruff problem crying in a living room, Perry knew that he was not actually "seeing" events as they happened. He did not have any super human powers (although the idea of having the ability to become invisible was very appealing and Perry thought a lot about how much fun it would be to walk unseen into a classroom and cause bloody havoc for his old teachers by making chalk and erasers seem to float just by carrying them around in his invisible hands, and about what a laugh would ensue when he would lift Mrs. Ferderko's long dress over her head, exposing her girdle for all the class to see, and about all the shit-heads that ever laughed at him or left him out of parties that he would smack and punch and kick), and Perry accepted this deficiency. Even if he couldn't physically get away, he wasn't about to imprison his mind in his immediate surroundings.

Perry saw Tanya pull into the Kentucky Fried Chicken parking lot (for real), and took a last haul from his cigarette. He crushed it beneath one greasy shoe. He exhaled as he sat down in the passenger seat. Despite the damaging affects of second hand smoke, Tanya patted Perry's knee and gave him a kiss on the mouth. Perry felt Tanya's lips, the lips of innocence, press gently against his own. He lingered in their velvety softness. He could not decide if her lips were wet or dry, so flawless was the balance between the two extremes. He wanted, needed, to open her mouth. He wanted to press his own lips, armed with the teeth behind them, against hers and, like a trained dog might whir its head to catch a snack placed on its snout, flick his head upward, working the lock of Tanya's top lip. He held himself back, though, suppressing the animal, knowing from experience that it was not for him to decide when the mouth of innocence, of beauty, should open. Their mouths parted without a sound, a silent smack, and Perry felt a small dynamite detonation in his chest when he saw a glittering strand of silky saliva caught between his bottom and her top lip. He tried in vain to follow Tanya's head as she pulled away from his, hoping to keep the flickering liquid bond between them intact. He felt the rope explode and basked in the tiny spray that washed against his chin, the sweet mélange of his own and Tanya's spit. Perry began to silently review strategies for getting more out of Tanya later on.

"I picked up your clothes at your house and you can take a shower at my house before we go," Tanya said.

"Thanks," Perry replied, a little distracted.

"Your brother still acts really weird around me."

"Brian or Greg?" Perry began to pay more attention.

"Greg. When I was waiting for your Mom to get your stuff he came up to me karate chopping and talking like an idiot."

"Was he making his mouth move all fast? Like, faster than he was really talking?"

"Yeah."

"That's his new thing. He's pretending to be a kung fu fighter in a dubbed movie."

"I know but it's weird."

"I'm not saying anything to him 'cause he's still bugging me about the last time I yelled at him about this crap. When you phoned and said 'Can I speak to Perry?', and he said 'I dunno, can you?', I gave him shit and now he says that I said that he's gonna be 'the cause of this breakup!' As if I ever said that."

"That's so cute!"

"I never said that!"

"I know, but it's cute."

Perry fumbled through the cassettes in Tanya's glove compartment. "Do you still have my White Stripes in here?"

"I'm listening to *my* music!"

"I'm pretty hungry, can you go through the Drive-Thru somewhere?"

"We're eating in like two hours and Michelle is making burritos."

"Wait, we're going to her place? I thought they were coming to your house."

"I told you we were going there. Didn't you listen to me?"

"Are your parents taking their own car?"

"Why, do you have to be home early? It's not like we're going downtown or anything. Your parents know it's just my aunt's house."

"It's not my parents...what if *I* want to leave early?"

"Then get your own car."

"Mm."

After a short ride during which the Indigo Girls did most of the rest of the talking, Tanya parked the station wagon in her parents' two-car garage. Just before going in the house, Perry squeezed her left buttock and received a playful swat on the hand for his effort, a sure sign that any lingering animosities had been left in the car. Mr. McMillen was in the living room reading a magazine with the television on. A British soap opera was playing, so Perry surmised that his girlfriend's father had been watching some other program on the same channel and simply hadn't bothered to turn off the set when it was over. "I guess some people don't know that the OFF button can be a choice," he thought to himself, laughing inside. This brief moment of superiority fizzled with the sound of Mr. McMillen's voice.

"Hi there, Perry. How are things at the KFC?"

"Just fine. We cooked some chickens today." It was a crude and uncomfortable attempt at a joke, but it was the only way Perry knew how to talk with the man, with the father of the girl he wanted to have sex with in a car before the day was over. Mr. McMillen offered a polite laugh. He immediately switched to a friendly sarcastic tone that matched Perry's, which was the best way he knew how to communicate with the kid whose tongue he suspected of being inside his daughter's mouth on numerous occasions. In this way, Perry and Tanya's father had been able to engage themselves in conversation for the past ten months or so without ever actually talking.

"Looks like your pants are a little dirty there, Perry."

Perry glanced down to see numerous streaks of white flour on the thighs of his navy blue polyester uniform pants. "Yeah, I know. It's just that this new guy kept wiping his hands on me today."

Mr. McMillen laughed again, this time even more politely. "Well, you better change before Tanya wipes her hands of you!"

Perry and Mr. McMillen forced themselves to smile and laugh until Tanya and her mother walked into the room. Tanya was carrying a large blue towel that she handed to Perry. "Here you go, babe." It was clean and smelled strongly of lemony fabric softener sheets, a foreign but pleasing scent to Perry. "We're going to the store to get wine while you take your shower."

"Um, are you all going?" Perry asked, deliberately blinking his eyes, hoping Tanya would understand the hidden, libidinous meaning behind his question.

"Yeah... I guess." Tanya looked confused, studying Perry's eyes.

"Well, it's just that—"

"Okay, let's go," Mr. McMillen suddenly ordered, rising from the couch with the magazine in his hand.

"Alright, Dad," Tanya replied. Her expression changed abruptly, a look of comprehension washing over her face. She winked at Perry, shrugged apologetically, and blew him a kiss as she followed her parents to the door. Perry pretended to catch the kiss on his cheek and lowered his head, exaggerating his dejection. Tanya laughed and shut the door. Perry turned the television off.

There was something exciting to Perry about being left alone in somebody else's house. It wasn't as good as having his very own place, tops on Perry's list of aspirations, but at least when nobody was home he didn't have to worry if his shirt was untucked or make sure there was a coaster under his glass. He wanted to smoke but doing so in the middle of the McMillen's living room was out of the question. He told himself to wait until later, in the shower, where the smoke would blend nicely with the steam in the bathroom fan and his cigarette butt could be disposed of without detection into the shower drain. First, however, Perry did as he usually did when he found himself unchaperoned in a house: head straight for the kitchen. "Just a little sandwich before they get back," he thought.

Opening up the McMillen's refrigerator, Perry was amazed, as he always was, by the quantity of food and incredible selection inside. At home, his own parents' fridge was filled with monstrosities: blasts from the past like six-month old taco sauce in a jar that was impossible to close properly because there was dry sauce caked all around its rim, or leftover spaghetti and meat balls in a cereal bowl that had turned orange and hard as rock because it had never been covered. In the McMillen's fridge, all leftovers and opened sandwich meat packages were carefully sealed inside ziplock bags, while in his own fridge at home Perry felt lucky if the ham was wrapped in paper towels.

Perry began to compile the necessary ingredients for his sandwich on the counter: cheese, lettuce, alfalfa sprouts, mortadella, pickles, tomato, turkey. He paused to consider the spreading condiments. He could have taken his usual combination of mustard and mayonnaise but he found a jar of Hellman's *Dijonnaise* spread, pre-mixed mustard and mayonnaise. Unable to decide, Perry grabbed all three jars. He then made his way to the opposite end of the kitchen counter where all the bread was kept in a basket. "Nobody ever has fucking sourdough," he thought as he checked out the selection. He opened a package of pumpernickel, took out two slices and turned back toward the fridge. Then he thought better of it and grabbed the rest of the loaf. "Something to snack on while I'm *making* the sandwich," he thought, reaching for the butter dish on the counter.

With a mouthful of butter-on-bread "snack", Perry took out the McMillen's cutting board and grabbed a steak knife. With nobody at home, Perry chewed with his mouth open and farted at will. He cut three thin slices of tomato and hid the rest at the bottom of the garbage can. Again farting and licking a finger, Perry opened the ziplock containing a fresh looking round of mozzarella cheese. "Saputo, no doubt," he thought and cringed at the memory of his own fridge stocked only with generic brand processed cheese slices. He cut himself a thick wedge of mozzarella. Taking another bite of his snack, Perry opened the jar of *Dijonnaise* spread and used the steak knife to distribute the product on a slice of pumpernickel. Perry spread a very thin layer of mustard on the other slice of bread and reached out for the grand prize. "Mmmm, mayonnaise," he said out loud in a deliberate Homer Simpsonesque voice.

After almost laughing at his own joke, Perry recalled staying home from school one day as a young boy, ailed by the sickness his parents liked to call "fake-itis," and watching Richard Simmons with his mother on morning television. Some of the members of the studio audience admitted to eating mayonnaise sandwiches in the past, and Richard berated them in a playful and loving way. He put his hands on his firm hips and shook his head in exaggerated disappointment. He then shook a school-teacher's finger at them and said, "That's very very bad bad bad!" He was smiling, though, and ready to love everybody and exercise, and Perry wished that Richard Simmons was his schoolteacher. That day, as soon as his mother went into the shower, Perry stole for the kitchen and made his very first mayonnaise sandwich. He had never realized that two slices of Wonder Bread with nothing but mayo between them could taste so divine, and he had continued the luscious habit into early adulthood. "Thank you Richard Simmons," Perry thought.

A sudden noise from outside made Perry jump. His heart began to pound and he held his breath for a moment. He hopped to the window over the kitchen sink and peered out, straining to see as much as possible. The driveway was empty but it was impossible from the angle to see inside the McMillen's garage. "They couldn't already be home," Perry thought. "Shit!" He took no chances, however, and began to hide all evidence of the raid he had made on the refrigerator; on food that he had not only failed to pay for but that he had never been given permission to touch. Perry launched the steak knife into the sink and grabbed the loaf of pumpernickel. "Where's the fuck-ing tie… where's the tie… oh shit." Perry fell to his knees and scoured the floor for any sign of the small piece of plastic. He swept his hands across every inch of tiling in his range, ignoring the dozens of tiny crumbs collecting on his sweaty palms, and con-tinued to talk to himself. "I'm going to look like such an idiot!" Finally, under the kitchen table, Perry found the tie and he sprung to his feet to continue the cover up. His fingers felt frostbitten as he fumbled to tie up the bread bag. "How am I ever going to face them?" he wondered. "Shit!"

He heard the slamming of car doors and knew only seconds remained for him to get out of the kitchen. He screwed the tops on the mustard, mayonnaise, and the Hellman's *Dijonnaise* and stuffed them into the fridge. In his mind's eye, Perry could see Tanya and her parents, getting out of the car, Mrs. McMillen holding a bag with the new bottle of wine in it, Mr. McMillen tinkering with something in the garage before going inside, and Tanya, his beautiful girlfriend, making her way to the house. "She's going to see me!" Perry was running out of time so he flung the lettuce, *mortadella,* pickle jar, alfalfa sprouts, and turkey back into the fridge and hid the unwrapped mozzarella at the bottom of the garbage can next to the unused portion of the tomato he had stolen. "I'm a fucking thief!"

With the muffled voices of the McMillen family growing closer and louder by the second, Perry brushed the bread crumbs and tomato residue off the cutting board with his hand, sucked the sorry excuse for *bruschetta* from his fingers, grabbed the uncompleted sandwich and the blue towel, and ran for the bathroom. He got the shower going immediately and stripped himself of his Kentucky Fried Chicken uniform. Perry was panting but enjoying the return of oxygen to his lungs along with the gradual alleviation of his fear and panic from the kitchen. "I made it…I can't believe I fucking made it," he muttered to himself. He looked at the sandwich in his hand. "If only I had put some turkey in first! Shit!" Resigned to the fact that his meal was nothing more than a glorified cheese sandwich with a few slices of tomato, a little mustard and some Hellman's *Dijonnaise* spread, Perry hopped into the shower. He pushed the nozzle straight down, so as to not wet his sandwich. "Christ, I could have had two of these if they hadn't came back so fast," he thought. "I won't even be able to smoke now!"

There was knocking at the bathroom door. "How's it going in there, babe?" Tanya asked.

"Just fine," Perry composed himself. "I just have to wash my bum." He heard Tanya giggle on the other side of the door.

A bar of soap on a small shelf almost directly beneath the shower nozzle succumbed to the water pressure and slipped into the tub. Perry's instincts told him to bend over immediately and pick up the bar since soap melted faster when exposed to water. His father had taught him that at an early age and concern for melting soap came as naturally to Perry as the impulse to get out of the way of a speeding car did. He thought of a joke his father had told him when he was young, probably around the same time that he learned about melting soap.

The two bears were taking a bath. One said to the other, "Please pass the soap." The other looked around and said, "No soap, radio!"

This was a joke designed to be a real joke on the listener. It was best told with a collaborator; someone who knew about the joke and would feign wholehearted laughter after the impotent "No soap, radio" punch line. If the listener was weak-minded enough to laugh along even though he or she did not "get" the joke, the joke teller and the collaborator could then laugh at the listener. Perhaps Perry's father was trying to teach his son a lesson about being a follower, about the pitfalls of going along with the crowd. He had miscalculated, however, since the image of two bears taking a bath together was genuinely funny to Perry's eight-year-old aesthetic sensibilities. He grew impatient and frustrated when his father attempted to explain why the joke was "really" funny. Since then Perry had been haunted by the lines of a very stupid joke every time he saw a bar of soap unnecessarily melting in water.

Perry turned his face away, leaving the soap bar to drown in the base of the tub, and began to concentrate on his pitiful sandwich. He pivoted so the water splashed on the back of his legs and took a bite. "Not enough mayo," he thought. Chewing with his mouth open, Perry looked the sandwich over. "Maybe Tanya will have sex with me in the car tonight," he thought. "Do I have enough cash, just in case, for the Motel Ideal?" Just then Perry spat out his half-chewed mouthful and gagged and coughed. It was not the thought of his girlfriend naked that made him act in such a disgusting manner, however. It was something about the sandwich. In his nonchalant inspection of the bread, Perry had discovered a horrifying defect.

Mould! Nauseated by the dusty green micro-organisms that had taken root on his sandwich and angered at the thought of having taken a terrible risk for nothing, Perry stomped one foot in the tub. Faced with the prospect of having to dispose of uneaten food, Perry heard the sound of his late grandmother's voice in his head. *Think of the poor, starving children in Cambodia, Perry.* He almost responded but shook himself back to reality. He had to get rid of the evidence but consuming it was now out of the question. There was a small garbage can in the washroom—perhaps he could hide it at the bottom of it as he had done with the cheese and tomato in the kitchen. But bathroom garbages never get changed, Perry pointed out to himself. He winced as a vision appeared in his mind of fruit flies hovering over the can and Mr. McMillen attempting to solve the mystery. Impulsively, Perry opened the shower curtain and plunked the sandwich into the toilet. He had one foot on the bath mat and one hand on the flusher when he realized that flushing a sandwich down the toilet not only stood a good chance of causing a blockage, but that it would also make his shower scalding hot for a few minutes. He reached into the toilet, withdrew the soppy molded sandwich, and returned to the shower.

Perry crouched down and began to break up the sandwich into little, olive-sized pieces. He placed each one into the tub's drain. He had to keep pushing the bar of soap aside, as the sucking action of the drain continuously drew it toward the hole. He waited a few seconds before depositing each new sandwich morsel into the hole to be sure the last one had really gone down. "I look like the most pitiful person on Earth," Perry said to himself. He thought about all the dead people he knew who might be watching him now as ghosts. As a youngster, he had always been compelled to curb his behaviour around his grandmother, but now that she was dead did that mean he had to be good all the time? "She couldn't be here now, I'm naked," Perry assured himself. He returned to the task at hand, hoping his plan would work. It took about five minutes to dispose of the entire sandwich, piece by piece, down the bathtub's drainpipe. There was another knock at the door.

"Almost done in there, Perry? We'd like you to be dry by the time we get to my sister's house." It was Mr. McMillen. Perry laughed out of courteous instinct but paranoia made him answer as one would a drill sergeant.

"Be out in a sec!"

Perry wet his hair and grabbed a plastic bottle of shampoo from the shelf beneath the shower nozzle. He quickly lathered his armpits with the triple action formula to alleviate some of the odour from his day's work, rinsed, and turned the water off. He stepped out of the shower and dried himself with the fluffy blue. Perry wondered what he was supposed to do with somebody else's towel after he had used it. At home, he simply placed his towels back on a hook and his mother would eventually put them in the wash when she felt they had been used enough. Here, though, nobody would be using the towel again before laundry day so he felt a little guilty about hanging it up in the bathroom. While his father had taught him many things about the physical properties of soap, he had failed to instill any sort of guest towel etiquette in his son. Perry had no choice but to hang the towel up but, out of politeness and consideration, was careful not to let it touch the other McMillen towels on the rack.

He put his good clothes on and left the bathroom. Mr. McMillen was still waiting outside and the two smiled uncomfortably at each other. Tanya appeared from around a corner and gave him a big hug around the neck. "Let's go in my room and do your hair," she said. She planted a big kiss on his cheek with her soft lips, wetting them on Perry's damp skin. "I like it when you comb it down." Perry was rigid, he felt ill at ease with one of Tanya's parents so close by. They began to walk down the hall.

The voice came from back inside the bathroom. "What did you do to my bath tub, Perry?" Mr. McMillen asked half-jokingly and half-annoyed. Perry was silent. He had no sarcastically friendly comeback for Tanya's father this time; he was unable to utter a word. "Looks like you blocked up my bath tub. It's full of water. Are you shedding or something?"

The sandwich! The plan hadn't worked and Mr. McMillen was on the verge of discovering Perry's act of robbery. In that moment Perry wished more than ever that his body could follow his mind to some remote town in Northern Manitoba where polar bears come in the spring to feast in the garbage dumps. Maybe he would be one of the lucky citizens to be interviewed by the reporters from the big cities who flocked annually to the town to take advantage of this cute human-interest story. Perry thought that he'd like to give his opinion that the yearly polar bear visit was nothing and it was the media invasion alone that caused the biggest disturbances to his little town for a few days every year. He wondered which television station would be brave enough to air his dissenting views on the matter. His body was firmly grounded in the McMillen hallway, however, and his continental wandering was cut off by the voice of the father of the house.

"Why don't you come in here and give me a hand unblocking this thing, Perry?" He wanted, needed, to run. He only stood there.

Tanya pushed him toward the bathroom. "Go and help him, babe."

"Better yet," Mr. McMillen began again, "you can go get my tool box from the garage. It looks like I might need a screwdriver or something to fish out whatever's blocking all this water."

"Why... why don't you just try some Liquid Drano or something, Mr. McMillen?" Perry practically pleaded.

"I don't like to put too much of that stuff into the pipes. It eats them all up."

Perry wouldn't have minded a little Drano to eat his own insides up at that moment. Anything would have been better than facing Mr. McMillen and Tanya once the remnants of his sandwich were extracted. There would be no way to explain it away. He made for the garage, hoping Tanya would stay with her father and he could run. Run away and never come back. Hiding was better than humiliation and there would be no humiliation as long as Perry was hiding. True to form, however, Tanya followed him to get her father's toolbox. "You don't mind helping him, eh Perry?"

"Ah, no. No, not at all." Perry thought he might push Tanya down and run, but he stopped himself. Doing that would mean giving up everything he had or would ever have with Tanya. He was torn. He feared the censure of the lips as much as he loved them. Why did he always do things like this?

They retrieved the toolbox together. It was a giant red thing made of metal with three sets of fold-out shelves and Perry felt it weighed a ton. The box boasted every tool a family could ever need: screwdrivers, hammers, pliers, and a giant wrench, perfect for taking pipes apart, to name but a few. There were even a few gems still wrapped in unopened packages: four extra bolts for keeping the toilet bowl connected to the floor, a tiny rock sculpting hammer, and a pair of UV-protective work goggles; every tool a family could never need.

Perry and Tanya made their way back to the washroom. Perry feared it might be the last thing they would ever do together. Mr. McMillen was sitting on the edge of the tub. Perry thought he might know already. He would have liked very much to use the toilet. "I don't know what the hell's in there. I can't see through this water, it's all murky." Relief. For the moment. Small beads of sweat tickled Perry's forehead and his hands shook slightly, causing the toolbox to rattle a bit. Tanya's father was frustrated and getting impatient, and he took it out on his daughter. "Tanya, are you helping or watching?" She looked surprised. "Will you please wait outside?" Tanya stomped off.

Now the men were alone. Time to roll up the sleeves and get to the bottom of things. Only Perry already knew exactly why the bathtub was blocked. The water would not go down because Perry had to have a little extra; he wasn't satisfied with what he was being offered; he had to have more. He had never been satisfied and probably never would. "And what did I get?" he asked himself, knowing the answer. "A mouldy sandwich with no mayo and no meats and a blocked tub to expose me." He felt a sudden urge to confess. Perhaps full admission of guilt before disclosure would at least gain Perry a little respect even if it did nothing for the shame.

The words were on the tip of Perry's tongue when Mr. McMillen got down on his knees with his back to him. He looked at the man's hunched shoulders and listened to the sounds of splashing water. "Just tell him, get it over with," Perry told himself. He grabbed the large wrench from the toolbox instead.

The small bald spot on the back of Mr. McMillen's head looked putty soft to Perry. He would not face the humiliation, he had to avoid it. It occurred to Perry, in the moment that he began to raise the wrench in the air, that Clue games don't have bathrooms. They have Halls, Conservatories, and Kitchens, and they certainly have Wrenches, but no Lavatories. Perhaps there were no famous crimes or murders that took place in a washroom to inspire the creators of Clue.

The wrench was high above Perry's head and he knew that running to a canning town in New Brunswick would be worth the trouble if he could prevent Mr. McMillen from discovering the dissected sandwich in his drain pipe. Living on the lam never looked so good to Perry and he actually began to look forward to his new life on the run. "I'll only have to be really careful for five, maybe six years," he thought. Perry felt the cold steel of the wrench handle press against the small bones in his fingers, felt the heat of straining tendons in his forearm as they struggled to keep the heavy tool aloft. He began to swing the wrench. "Will it crack? Will it crunch?" he wondered.

A terrifically loud sucking sound suddenly filled the air in the bathroom. It startled Perry so much that he missed his target, struck himself on the knee, and dropped the wrench onto the back of Mr. McMillen's left calf. Perry slumped to the ground, his right kneecap throbbing. Mr. McMillen let out a sharp yelp and scrambled to his feet. The sucking didn't stop and Perry thought for a second that his grandmother was returning from the dead to tell him how naughty he had been and that there would be no more chocolate bars until his behaviour changed. Mr. McMillen returned Perry to the reality of his surroundings: "God dammit! What are you fooling with a wrench for, Perry?"

Perry ignored his girlfriend's father's words. He only listened to the sucking and swishing sounds that he now realized were emanating from the tub. Mr. McMillen was sweating and screaming and waving one arm in the air, but his words were no more discernible to Perry than the speech of the schoolteacher in Peanuts television cartoon specials. The sweet sucking. That was what Perry was interested in. "The...the water! Is it going down?" Perry cried.

Mr. McMillen rubbed the back of his leg. "Yes it's going down, you klutz!" He threw a small bar of wet soap at Perry. "There's the problem. There's the damned blockage. A piece of soap. Don't you put the soap back when you're finished? Oh, my leg!"

Perry felt giddy with relief. It was as if he had just finished a ten-hour shift in the Kentucky Fried Chicken kitchen and had the next two weeks off. He shuffled to his good knee to watch the last swirl of water sink down into the drain. It looked like a tiny tornado. "It's okay? The tub's okay?"

"The tub's okay. The tub's okay," Mr. McMillen mocked, imitating the frenzy in Perry's voice. He wondered why Perry was so distraught but attributed it to his prior conviction that the boy was simply strange. "The tub's okay but soap isn't cheap, you know. It melts a hell of a lot faster if you leave it in the water. Don't you think you could be a little more careful there, Perry?"

Perry eyed the fallen wrench again as he stood up. He gripped it. He handed it to Mr. McMillen. The man shook it at Perry, feigned a swing in the air, and smiled.

No soap radio.

JAMIE POPOWICH

TOMMY LE VAN MEETS THE BABIES

They'd been arguing late one night when Tommy said, "Well, I'm not sure that all these things have to be decided right now." Trudy responded, "Fine. But when will it be okay to be serious? Or are we always going to have to pretend there's nothing serious? Should we just wait to talk about serious things like marriage or having a baby, till we're fifty, and it's too late to worry about it? Is that how you want to do things?"

"Babies? We're not even talking about babies."

"Well maybe we should."

Maybe we should. The words that activated the bomb which went off without warning in every subsequent fight. Maybe we should. Ka-Boom! If Tommy didn't think it was important before, after those three words had been uttered for the first time, he quickly realized how dangerous babies could be. They were these grenades being lobbed into the air in little white diapers with one or two pieces of hair on their head, their hands outstretched to him, making incomprehensible noises. He tried to imagine catching one but could only picture himself, in vain, trying to juggle one of these slippery little people as it wriggled, screamed, and fell its way to a mess on the floor. He no longer saw himself as the person his mother so glowingly described as being, "great with kids."

Why didn't they talk about marriage or buying a house, ideas that seemed more practical to him than having a child. Trudy didn't want to though, because when it came down to it, she didn't believe he wanted to have children.

Tommy didn't know how to answer her. He wanted to say how could someone like him, someone who is trying to create a life for himself, could ever take responsibility for creating and maintaining someone else's life? He, who couldn't even tie his shoelaces the sophisticated way, but instead made two loops then crossed them over and around each other. A manner which he was told by the next door neighbour, as she showed him, at seven years of age, was for people who didn't have the knack to understand the other way, a way which by now he'd forgotten, let alone ever understood. And suddenly, he would have to start thinking about teaching another person how to do it as well. Where was his neighbour, the girl who had grown up, moved away, and now had two kids of her own? Would it be too late to call her up and ask her to show him and his new, fictional kid, how to do up their laces again? "Uh hi. Um, we used to be neighbours, and I think you may have had a crush on me, but, uh, that's not important, well, would you mind coming over and showing me and my new baby how to do up our shoes? Hello? Hello?"

Now babies were all over the place. It's as if, at the mere mention of them, they'd suddenly grown tall enough to reach his eye level. He liked it better when they stayed around his ankles and he could just step over them unaware. But whatever he did now seemed to include babies. Every time he turned on the television people were trying to have babies. There were real-life births, fictional births, couples talking about births. When he went to order a coffee once, he was crunched between two babies in slings attached to their mothers' chests. Outside, he was constantly avoiding oncoming baby carriages, which barreled toward him. And in his apartment, the only refuge he had left, the sound of a baby wailing could be heard coming through the walls, ceilings, and floor. To him this was the battle cry, the sound of the bugle before he and Trudy would begin fighting again.

Sure he'd thought of having a kid, not seriously, but he'd thought "Yeah I guess that'll happen." He remembered being ten and actually thinking proudly about having a child and how happy his parents would be when he brought home their grandchild (because, of course, at ten, he still imagined living with his parents). That fantasy must have been forced on his little ten year old mind by all the baby propaganda. The billboards, the sitcoms, the people who always asked him at what age he planned to have kids, as if it were already predetermined.

In fact, the majority of the time he imagined having a baby as the defeat of his life. He'd have no choice but to live with his parents because he'd have no money. He'd work several low paying jobs with crotchety managers who always looked over Tommy's shoulder, tapping his watch, making Tommy apologize for his existence, and saying: "I hope your kid isn't as big a screw-up as you are Le Van." This scenario Tommy called "Feeding the Baby."

Other equally fearsome baby dreams included "Slobbering baby in restaurant", "All my friends are going out but me", "No sex", "No sleep", "Out too late with evil boys", "Drugs" (the last two being future prophesies of the teenage years).

What was even worse for Tommy was the idea of the actual pregnancy. Those nine supposedly exciting months when the mother of his kid got bigger and bigger. Tommy imagined a time where he would be expected to be on call at all hours, two beepers, and a cell phone with a loud ring, attached to his belt. Every time one of these emergencies went off he'd have to drop everything and run and get pickled ice cream, or help lift her up from a restaurant chair, or rub her swelled feet. Tommy never understood those men who said, "If I could do it I would." Tommy was sure these guys would have given birth to a baby even if it meant the thing had to come out their penis. They would probably love to watch as their little dinks grew to a size they'd be proud of, saying the whole time, in between passing out, "isn't creation beautiful?"

But he wouldn't be the one giving birth; it'd just be his responsibility to make sure everything else about the birth worked. He didn't even have a driver's license though, and would probably end up involved in one of those cab births. If that didn't happen then no doubt he'd forget all that he learned at the Lamaze classes as his hand got squeezed by the soon-to-be-mother. There was also the fact that he'd have no idea what to talk with the woman about while all this was going on (would sports be inappropriate? Fashion?).

What Tommy most feared about the birth was the baby finally, miraculously, arriving, only to be developmentally challenged in some way. He'd heard that most parents' knee jerk reaction is one of sickness. They don't want it, they won't love it. Apparently, the hospital makes them tape their initial responses and then plays it back to them a few months later, at which time the parents can hear how absolutely horrible they used to be. Because, of course, they'll change their minds. How could they not? This was their little baby. Theirs and nobody else's. And when it comes down to it, that baby, even if at first it seems different from normal, really is as normal as every other supposedly normal child. Look at all the screwed up, supposedly normal people in the world, Tommy always thought. No there was no difference in the end. This was the lesson he was sure that he'd learn. But what if he didn't want to? What if after all was said and done, he was one of those people who told the doctors and nurses to take the child away because he wasn't strong enough to deal with that in his life? What if he did that?

He didn't like to think about this scenario. Most of the time he thought about how his whole life would be about his new baby. Tommy would slowly, happily, lose his space on the bed, until he was offering to sleep on the floor. Blankets, pillows, no you keep them, the baby needs them, he'd say. No, by the time his little piece of life was in his arms, smiling from gas, he'd be totally lost. Tommy? Tommy who? That loser's gone now. Life is just about this new Beautiful Funny Genius Le Van. Everything Tommy did would be for the kid. There'd be no more dream of owning a bar, and really how could there be? A bar, full of alcoholic, broken-hearted, pavement pushing, defeated patrons, was no kind of example for a child in its formative years. And that's not even taking into consideration the damage that all that cigarette smoke would do to those precious lungs, or the sight of those gaping maws slugging back the devil's juice. The kind of child who grew up in that would later be telling the judge, "By six I was taking nips from all the booze lying around, not that my dad noticed.

He was too busy busting his ass for every dime he could get. By the time I was seven I was peddling broads. And by eight, whoa, I don't remember eight so hot." Tommy couldn't ever risk the possibility of that coming true. So his dream of owning a bar would have to be thrown out the window.

Which he didn't want to do. He didn't want to negotiate having a life and having a baby. No matter how amazing the sight of a baby coming out a woman's vagina looked on television, and he always loved the sight of the baby being raised in the air for the first time, what he loved even more was the distance he had between that image and himself. That made the moment even better. Because that wasn't his baby, his responsibility. He wasn't the one who'd have to be up thirty times a night making sure the baby was still breathing, changing its diapers, feeding it, or rocking it. Someone else would be doing that and he'd never have to think about it.

This is the way he felt about babies. The problem arose when he had to verbalize it to Trudy. When he heard her say, "What about babies?" he wanted to drop all this in front of her and say, "Here's what!" He never could though. If he did, Trudy would be out the door, busy labeling him as "anti-human" to the press. She'd think that the real reason he didn't want kids was because it interfered with his social life and his sex life. She'd think the idea of a pregnant woman disgusted him, but that wasn't true. He'd thought a few times about spooning with a pregnant woman and being able to reach around a lay his hand on that huge belly, not a fat belly, but the belly that surrounded a second person. And then there were those huge milk-filled breasts. He imagined that could be lots of fun as well.

But really when it came down to it, the pregnancy, the birth, the runny noses, packed lunches, teachers' meetings, and everything else that went into being a parent didn't appeal to him. It was as simple as that (at least in his mind).

It was not normal though for the people walking down the street and pushing baby carriages in front of them. Not for those people. To them he was just avoiding his responsibilities because he was scared of growing up, scared of taking chances. Because for them it was simply impossible that someone would want to live their life without a baby.

ROBERT PRIEST

HOW TO SWALLOW A PIG

Because of the shape of its face, a pig is actually one of the easiest animals to swallow whole.* Still, pig-swallowing is a very difficult and potentially dangerous activity. If you have advance notice, a certain amount of jaw-stretching and lip-widening prior to the event is always helpful. Your greatest enemy is self-doubt. You have to look at the pig's head and tell yourself that you can do this. Once you have greased the pig, begin by letting the fine tapered end of the snout proceed through your lips. The first obstacle, if it is not the back of your throat, will likely be your front teeth. Unfortunately these will have to be broken off. This clears the way for the full face-taper of the pig snout to zero in on your gullet. You have to be thinking "outrage" when this begins to happen for it is entirely violating and painful. But your throat can take it. Allow the gorge to widen as though it were a fluid, thinner with each stretch. You throat is a powerful python, infinitely elastic and accommodating. Once the entire pig head has squeezed by your gag reflex and entered your gorge you are fully committed. You will not be able to vomit out the pig safely. Nor can you wait long to continue, for at this time your trachea is entirely blocked by the pig's head. You are unable to breathe. Do not panic. Do not attempt to gasp or retch. Concentrate on swallowing. Having the wideness of the pig's bulky shoulders in your once narrow throat is perhaps the most violating thing you will ever experience. But you can do this. Just tell yourself: this is possible. Swallow and stretch. Keep your lower jaw loose to prevent the bone from snapping at the hinge. Suck with your guts. Use your lower diaphragm to draw the fat pig ever further down the gullet. Let your thick and lucent saliva lubricate the way. Saturating the pig with your juices will allow the celiated gorge to usher the pig deeper and deeper into your being. You may now need a friend with a stick to stuff in the pig's back end. This is the most crucial period. You will have been without oxygen for quite some time. You are probably blue in the face, but if you can widen to your most extreme limit, your throat cracking like wet bark, you will be able to slide your blue lips over the bare buttocks and with the last kick of the back trotters, the curl of the pig's tail will be gone. The entire pig is in your throat. Your intestines are stretching. Peristalsis has begun. The glottis is finally released and the first, terrible new breath can come with a gasp. You've lived! You've swallowed the whole pig. And now that it's entirely in your stomach you have to ask yourself: Is this not a most familiar feeling? Is this not the greatest feeling on earth?

---

* It is also one of the easiest animals to shove up the anus. This is not recommended for reasons of hygiene.

INSTRUCTIONS FOR LAUGHTER

It is not proper to go "HA! HA!", open-mouthed, squinty-eyed, pointing. Laughing can be executed with perfect grace, elegance, and still be 100 percent expressive. Laugh with a straight spine. Let the *kundalini* energy come straight up and have its own little dance in the beauty of your face. Don't use laughing to shiver out disgust at your world, your self, whatever lies are coiling too tight that night. Don't use laughter to sneak some grief out. Don't make hollow "Aaaw Aaaaaw" or "Eeee-Eeee" sounds just to rattle some subterranean bit of the unused muscle of love. Don't stuff your laugh with terror bits. Don't push up a ragged laugh at outrage or half-turn a laugh that ends in shock or shame. Don't laugh in a high voice like a puppy when you don't mean it. A laugh is not a bag you carry out the psychic trash in. You must not laden it with death-dread and toxic, boxy bits of brokenness. Let your body be a tickled trumpet-tit to the laughter. Let the giddy laughter play you like a tongue in the heart till you're undone. Laugh till your genitalia are laughing too. Let each vein mouth laugh. But do not brazenly bend over with your hands on your knees and scream. Real laughter can occur at volumes well below 12-14 db. It is uncommon for evolved laughter to continue into weeping, but this on occasion can and does occur. In such instances it is proper to wipe tears only with one hand, the funny hand. (Decide which hand is funniest and let it wipe the tears.) It is considered vulgar to seek out laughter. It must come in the accidental course of living. Only this is true laughter. And so it is not proper to attend so-called comedy clubs, church services, or any reading, anywhere, of sacred vows.

STUART ROSS

THE PRESIDENT'S COLD LEGS

The president fell into the river and his legs got cold and he ended up in a wheelchair. I was pushing him along the sidewalk and someone with lots of shopping bags stopped us and said, "Did you know that's the president you're pushing there in that wheelchair?" Well, sure I knew—this was the president with the cold legs.

Later on, in my room, I wrote in my notebook: "The president likes how I push him along the sidewalk." Then I put my pencil down and waited for the phone to ring again. Whenever they needed me to push the president in his wheelchair they would phone me up and I would go to his house. I noticed that the wallpaper up near the ceiling was beginning to peel. I'd tell the president about that the next time I pushed him along the sidewalk. I mean, he wouldn't fix it himself, because of his cold legs and all, but he'd send someone to stick my peeling wallpaper back up.

And also my pencil was worn down to just about a stub. I hoped maybe he could get me a new pencil. He would say, "I will give you money for a new pencil because of how good you push me on the sidewalk." We'd stop outside a drugstore and he'd give me a handful of change and tell me to go in and buy a new pencil. I don't like to leave him alone like that but he says he's safe because he's a good president and everyone likes him.

Aside from pushing the president along on the sidewalk, I do other things too. At night, I sleep. Also, when I was a little boy I took my dog Rufus for walks, but not with a wheelchair. Rufus sniffed the back ends of other dogs that other boys were walking. I got a B in geography once. In the school band, we played a song called "Suicide Is Painless", which was the song they played on a TV show that everyone watched then. My father really liked that show a lot, and later he jumped off a big building, so I don't know what that means. Like most subjects, history was not my best subject at school, and sometimes when I push the president in his wheelchair I get scared he'll ask me a question where I have to know who was another president in history. I tried once to memorize the names of every president, but all I could remember was spumoni, because it was hot and I wanted ice cream.

Once at the post office, I was standing in line to buy some stamps and a man with a little hat came over and did a dance in front of me. It lasted a long time, and when it was finished he said, "Will you hire me now?" which probably meant would I hire him to do a dance. But I needed my money for stamps and I couldn't afford it. Later, when

I was pushing the president along the sidewalk, I asked him if he wanted to hire the man with the little hat to do a dance for him. He didn't say words, he just laughed, and I laughed too, but I didn't know why we were laughing.

Every year I have a birthday, but no one told me when I started, so I don't know how old I am. I don't know whether I am younger or older than the president. I think that I am younger, though, because he calls me "son." If I was older, he would call me "father." One time when it was my birthday, the president gave me a tape recording. He said that the man on the tape was a man named Hank Williams, and he liked him best of all singers, and that I reminded him of Hank Williams. I stopped pushing the president's wheelchair for a moment and I looked at the picture of the man on the tape. He had a cowboy hat on, but I wasn't wearing a hat. The president must have made a mistake. When I got home that day, I tore the plastic paper off of the tape recording, which I had to use my teeth to do. I went to the door of my next-door neighbour who is a nice woman with very big teeth and a blue dress and I asked her if she could play the tape for me because I don't have a tape recorder. She said okay and that I should come in and sit down. Then she put the tape the president gave me for my birthday in her tape recorder and she asked me where I got the tape. "The president with the cold legs," I told her, and just as I said that we heard music, just like those were the magic words that made the tape start singing. Me and the nice woman listened to the whole tape of Hank Williams and then we listened to it again. "He seems very sad," the woman said to me.

In my room I lay in my bed and thought about sadness and how I feel sorry for people who are sad. I wondered why people would feel sad if it makes them so sad. I tried to make myself sad by thinking about that my parents were dead and that I didn't know how old I was and that my pencil was really short and that if the president's legs hadn't gotten so cold when he fell in the river, he'd be able to walk like normal people. But nothing made me feel sad. Sometimes when I push the president along the sidewalk I can see that he is sad, but he doesn't sing songs like Hank Williams that sound like he's crying. I push his wheelchair faster so that he will have fun and I tell him funny stories about my dog Rufus. For example, sometimes when I walked him he would smell the back ends of other dogs that other boys were walking. Plus, when he got killed by the car in front of our house my father held him up by his rear legs and it looked like he was smiling, the way his tongue hung out of his mouth.

You shouldn't fall in a river because the river makes your legs cold and then you can't walk and I will have to push you around in a wheelchair along the sidewalk. And I don't really have time for that because I have to push the president and when I'm not pushing him, I have to sit in my room and look at my phone until somebody somewhere else dials my number and makes it ring.

When the president turns dead because the cold goes up from his legs into his heart, I will have to be the president. I will sit in his wheelchair and a man will push me along the sidewalk. When the man's pencil gets so short he can't even hold it or fit it into the sharpener, I will give him money to buy a new pencil. "Faster—push me faster," I'll yell when I'm sad. Then I'll point at a rock on the ground and say, "We sure are moving faster than that rock."

Maybe when I am the president, I will know how to be sad. With a pencil I will write a book about rocks and about sadness. When my pencil gets short, a man will bring me another pencil. My friends from school, although I did not have any friends at school, will come and visit me in my house. I will have a tape recorder when I am the president, and I will play my Hank Williams tape that the president gave me. I will tell my friends, "The president gave me this tape. When I pushed him along the sidewalk I looked like Hank Williams, even if I didn't wear a hat." And then my friends which I don't have will say how sad Hank Williams sounds. And I'll say that I know what they mean, because I will be the president.

ME AND THE POPE

It was one of those summers when people just kept coming to stay, and I'd pull out the futon and slap on the sheets and set my friends up in the living room. My place was small, and the overcrowding really bugged my girlfriend, who was far more solitary than me. There'd be a breather of two or three days before each new onslaught, and we knew that in a couple of months, the visits would all be history. But then the Pope called, and I couldn't really turn him down. He was coming to Toronto for a few days, and he'd be pretty busy, but he wanted somewhere to crash at night, and he remembered my futon fondly from years past. I told him yeah, okay, but I couldn't spend a lot of time with him—my girlfriend and I needed to reacquaint ourselves—and he was fine with that. So I went to the hardware store and cut him a key (Clint had left without giving back the extra), and told him I'd leave it for him in the mailbox.

The Pope wasn't great with stairs, and I was on the second floor, but he said he could manage. I was scared I'd come home one day and he'd be halfway up, sitting on his papal ass, his head hanging down at his chest, gasping for breath. I talked to my girlfriend and said at least one of us would have to be around to check in on him, and she agreed, but through gritted teeth. I looked forward to at least one late night of drinking and watching videos, when maybe I could turn the sound down low and talk to the Pope about the whole girlfriend thing. He was good about that, even though he didn't have a girlfriend himself. I figured that's what gave him perspective. I was worried that the Pontiff and my girlfriend wouldn't get along—they were complete opposites. In fact, I'd never had a girlfriend during any of his previous visits; he'd always show up when I was a bachelor, and he, of course, was a perpetual bachelor.

Things were pretty busy in the days leading up to his arrival, not only in the rest of the city, where they were putting up statues and shit, and making sure the Popemobile routes were secure, but also in my apartment. I was cleaning like a fiend. Usually, if a friend stayed for only a day or two, I wouldn't bother laundering the sheets, figuring the next arrivals would never notice. But the Pope was pretty picky about that—he had an amazing sniffer and always knew when I was slacking on the laundry. So I washed all the sheets, and threw out mouldy things from the fridge, and put away all the CDs that littered my living room, and made sure I had enough extra pillow cases (he liked three pillows for his head, and one between his knees when he lay on his side). I did some shopping, too, making sure there was plenty to eat. He was pretty good about that stuff—after he'd leave, I'd always find a can of peas or a bag of chips that he'd bought and stashed in my kitchen. He'd never taken advantage of me, that was for sure. And he did the dishes every morning—I'd wake to the clinking of plates and cutlery and yell from my bedroom for him to cut it out, I'd look after it, but His Holiness just shouted back that he *liked* to do it—they never let him at the Vatican.

The Pope's always full of surprises, and when he suggested one night that we knock over a convenience store, I did a double-take. He had a mischievous twinkle in his eye as he held up the keys to the Popemobile and shrugged his shoulders (the Pope was all shoulders). I cracked open another beer for myself and mulled it over. He was just staring at me, waiting for my answer, or perhaps he'd fallen asleep with his eyes open—it was always hard to tell. I told him to hold on, I just had to use the can, but instead of going to the washroom, I went into my bedroom, phoned my girlfriend, and asked what she thought of the idea. She didn't think too long before she declared it stupid, even if it had emanated from the Pope. I said, but come on, this is the Pope, he just wants to have some fun, he knows what he's doing, and she said it was crazy, and if I did it she'd leave me, because there's no way she was ever going to bail me out of jail again. I called her a bad Catholic and hung up on her. Then I punched my pillow in anger, or perhaps because it was flattened out, I don't remember, but either way, I immediately regretted breaking up.

Back in the living room, the Pope was watching Seinfeld on TV with the sound off and listening to a Yardbirds CD. I said, come on, man, let's just do it, and I reached for his keys. The Pope looked at me for a moment, his head on that weird angle, but his eyes as alert as ever. I thought he was going to frown and roar *Silencio* like he did in Nicaragua just before he yanked out all those liberation theology bishops, but he just laughed and tossed his keys in the air. He told me he'd been kidding, what was I thinking, he was the Pope, and then he turned back to the TV.

So the guy comes to town, crashes on my futon, watches my TV, and wrecks my relationship with my girlfriend. I kicked him out without a moment's hesitation, and hit the sack. I was exhausted. I mean, I'd done the laundry and cleaned up—I was bushed. In the morning, I turned on the TV. There was the Pope, in front of like 500,000 people, droning on and on about this and that, while people cheered and waved flags, and there was my girlfriend on his arm. That's what you get for being hospitable. I was going to call this "The Pope Stole My Girlfriend," but I didn't want to give everything away.

*U*NTITLED

It got me so furious when I went with Geoff to Rock On!, the record store. Buyer, manager and owner, M—who claimed his sister was David Bowie's latest girlfriend —would make deals with Geoff to trade records for fish. Geoff worked in a tropical fish store. These tiny and colourful aquaticforms had a market value of hundreds of dollars—each. What a scam! So Geoff would order the rarest of The Cure British pressings and sneak fish out of the aquariums into little Glad sandwich baggies filled with salt-water. Pre-surveillance days. Then we'd boot it downtown to Crescent street with the stolen goods.

I didn't give a shit about his stealing. Whatever. I got furious because Mr. Bigshot Owner would never fucking look at me when i went in with Geoff to bring his fish.

What am I, invisible? Hardly so. In that era—orange electrical hair socket and tight black spandex. Hardly so. He was just a sexist bastard. He took me for Geoff's girlfriend so kept his eyes averted. If he couldn't pick me up, he wouldn't even bother saying hello. Prick. He was ugly too. And old (30 at least?).

Was his sister better looking than him or did David Bowie just have bad taste?

*

The top two started poking out. The bottom two were impacted. And in a month's time I would have all four wisdom teeth yanked out of my head to the sweet sounds of the mixed tape that Geoff just made for me. Good timing. Dr. Sokoloff—dental surgeon to all the suburban eleventh grade stars—advised against waiting any longer. Something about messing up all the expensive work already done to my already fixed and perfect teeth. More probably something about paying for his daughter's private school tuition. At my first appointment in his sixth floor Côte-des-Neiges medical building office, he told me about the marathon he was training for. What is it with doctors and marathons? Melissa's dad—well, a pharmacist—was also a running fanatic. I mean, a fanatical runner. And skinny, just like Sokoloff.

Local anaesthetic, and with his bare hands he went in. Headphones clasped on ears pumping too loudly against the delicate drum—could not be a better solution to blocking out the picks, sprays and drills. I hate going to the dentist. Why not state the obvious? And this tape was amazing! 90 minutes of pre-spring anthems; Bauhaus' *Bela Lugosi's Dead* followed by Modern English's *Face of Wood* and The Glove's *Perfect Murder* (a brief Cure side-project). It went on and on. Ethereally chanted themes of after-life, paralysis and death swiftly replacing anxiety provoked by physiological sensations of after-life, paralysis and death. I am one with my music. My head hurts.

I never did call Sokoloff to thank him or to tell him that I had just contracted mononucleosis.

*

Seth, Steph, and Geoff came to visit me. Never showing an unmade face or undone hair in public, I wasn't too thrilled with them witnessing my in-bed-for-two-weeks-look. But oh, I was thrilled with the get-well gift they brought me—*Louder than Bombs*, a new Smiths double album!

In my transition from tooth-pulling recovery to full blown mono (why does my head feel like a bowling ball? Why is my tongue red swollen bumpy and killing me and why do I have lumps that look like cottage cheese growing at the back of my throat?) I maintained a steady Percocet high. Geoff put on the record while Steph played air drums and I looked at Seth—perched coyly on the edge of my bed. I realized I hadn't seen him since just before my mouth surgery. Good timing. During that last visit I had just come out of the shower and, sitting on the floor of my mother's room, licked his thighs and cock while he blew my hair with mom's hair dryer. What a babe! He looked like Morrissey. Sort of. I made Seth promise not to tell Geoff. I knew Geoff would be jealous and I was never deliberately hurtful.

Morrissey yodeled and we squealed. Some girl named Amelia barked orders in the living room at her production assistants. They were shooting Super-8 for a first year CEGEP film class. Who was that again? Oh yeah, my friend Katie's friend from school.

It was an April Saturday mid-afternoon and I hadn't moved since my morning pee.

Who let all these people in and where the hell was my mother?

*

Yes, Mom gave me my life and yes, Morrissey saved me/my life but still—

my two biggest late-adolescent long-lasting revelatory disappointments
(in no particular order):
1) Adults *do not* have their shit together and
2) Morrissey *is* a total wanker.

I missed some earlier opportunity to catch this irreverent genius in concert. I had
only just started listening to the Smiths when they came on their mid-80s tour and
hard-earned money selling trendy accessories was better spent on a drunken club
night than a potentially lame-ass live show.

This time Geoff and I had tickets and though we weren't convinced that the venue
was right—a school auditorium? who booked this?—we had to go. We would have
bought tickets to see the Smiths play in an underground sewer, we were that desper-
ate. I mean, that enamoured with this brilliant British band.

The opener—a small-boned folk-singer—got booed off the stage. Somehow, this
karmically didn't bode well. I smelled danger. Whatever. I was too excited to worry
about fate and finally, there they were, our beloved Smiths. The audience cheered, the
band started to play and Morrissey looked like he could barely stay standing. Does a
man who professes the carnage of carnivorous consumption consume recreational
drugs? Or maybe he had the flu?

No matter. The audience shrieked. Girls my age with hair and clothes just like mine
but with 3 times the courage pushed their way to the front of the hall and—

"Holy shit—there's a girl on stage throwing her arms around Morrissey! That could
be me! But it's not. And now she's being thrown off stage by a bouncer. Ouch. That
could be me. But it's not—holy shit, there's another one! And Morrissey is so out of
it that he's just hanging on to her face for dear life. Oh—there's the bouncer again,
ripping Morrissey's arms off of her face to toss her back to the crowd—oh there's
another one! And another! And another! Oh my god, they're rushing the stage—

Geoff, look at that, there's like, 25 girls up there and only 3 bouncers! They've totally lost control!"

And then to my HORROR, right before the first chorus of *Heaven Knows I'm Miserable
Now*—the two lines from the song I had been WAITING TO HEAR MY WHOLE
LIFE—the SOUND WAS CUT. AAARGH!!!

I burst into tears, girls screaming everywhere, bouncers and all the university staff
security running amuck.

And the grand fucking finale—

Morrissey being carried out on a stretcher.

The whole show lasted all of 15 minutes.

Hello? WHAT THE FUCK JUST HAPPENED?!?

After being ungraciously ushered out by rude campus police we contemplated chasing down the ambulance. But everyone else had the same idea too.

Depressed, we got on the next metro and made ourselves obnoxious to other pas-
sengers. Over to Stanley Street and the Thunderdome, we moped on a sticky dance
floor to the *Queen is Dead*. I guess somebody told the DJ.

Did I feel like a winner and I NEVER bought another Smiths album again.

*

and was the end of highschool alterna-goth downtown nightclub dance

and the beginning of dreadlocked dep wine balcony salad bar romance

KINDERGARTEN ART CRITIQUES

#1

<u>Day at the Zoo</u>   Theo Brown, Age 6

Magic Marker and Graphite

This piece should be called "I Am A Total Sham Artist With No Insight." Please, Theo. How transparent could you be? Everybody knows your frowning little animals in cages are just frowning little Theos in cages. Where is your imagination? Is it also trapped in a cage? Is it frowning? Is your imagination frowning, Theo? Let's try a little exercise. Imagine that bus represents your future as a successful artist. See all those little kids inside it? Think of them as your ideas. Now close your eyes and get ready. Okay. Ready? Are you picturing it? Now, imagine the bus driver stepping on to the bus and turning on the ignition and driving far, far away. Get it?

#2

<u>Fire Day</u>   Miranda Hersh, Age 6

Wax Crayon

Miranda doesn't get layout. Miranda has a narrative problem. Is the dog supposed to be the fireman? Because if I was in a fire, I wouldn't trust a dog to save me. Especially a floating dog without any feet. And what's with this composition? Miranda, the houses are on top of the girl and the dog which are on top of the fire truck. Is this supposed to be a dream? Is the fire supposed to be symbolic? Is this supposed to be a surrealist expression of sexual urgency? Are the absent firemen supposed to represent our society's lack of male authority figures? Please, Miranda. Your skewed perspective bores and even offends me. All in all this is a fragmented and superficial piece of garbage. Very amateur.

#3

<u>Plane</u>   Thomas Cooper, Age 5

Pencil Crayon and Aquarelle

First of all, Thomas' inaccurate depiction of parachutes displays a rather sophomoric belief about gravity. Listen sweetheart, heavy things don't float, Ok? Thomas also needs to learn the ways in which a true artist portrays direction and movement. Those vertical lines next to the parachute are supposed to show you that the parachuters are going down. Right, well, Thomas—most of us understand that. What we don't understand is how that plane is flying on its side. Furthermore, apart from a clear lack of technical ability, Thomas' work is fundamentally insulting. Note the lack of female representation in a work that embraces a male-identified world of technology. Oh, look, some MEN and a PLANE! Thank you, Thomas, for wowing me with your utterly innovative observations. You know what would be really unique? If maybe those women on the ground could go wash some dishes. Or bake you an apple pie. Would you like that Thomas? I bet you would, you small-minded misogynist.

#4

<u>My Apartment Building</u>   Robbie Bennett, Age 6

Oil Pastel and Graphite

These are rather mundane aesthetic choices aren't they? Don't you think this piece could use a little bit of, oh, I don't know... talent? Robbie is clearly attempting to capture the banality of his existence. If the intention behind this work is to hit us over the head with his see-through self-indulgence and commonplace symbolism then he has succeeded. And yet, isn't it peculiar that by succeeding he has failed?

REAL DOLL

Things you can be beside yourself with:

1) A sudden (ejaculatory) mood. (Example: I was beside myself with bliss or grief.)
2) A reasonable facsimile of yourself.

(Example: Bypassing the violent intrusion of bliss, slip out of body (out of mind) in a game of musical chairs (musical bodies), and enter (as vicarious site) she of the rigid apertures, the fixed and stable holes—who could perform your anxiety (performance anxiety) for you, leaving what is left of you to have a *latte,* perhaps.)

Sometime after Kiva and Dr. No, but before Bellamy and the ad hoc insertion of a video store guy, I know I want to purchase (or be made into) the perfect companion in the form of a real doll.

Real dolls resemble the liberal humanist conception of "people" (only they are almost always female, and are made out of plastic, and so, don't talk back). For an extra fee, you may have their heads custom made to look like someone you are stalking. I decide to have my own head put on the real doll. For purposes of verisimilitude, I consider buying her used (on eBay).

I am dubious about the used doll at first. As Wayde points out, yes, "that would be fine the first time you lend her out, but after that, who'd want to borrow her?" But then, bodies always come used. (Consider the places a mouth has been before the "first" kiss).

Also necessary, the paraphernalia of documentation (a Polaroid and video camera). Once equipped, I would lend her to serial persons of interest. In this way, she would collect to herself a story I could not fully know, but would be invested in, literally, through deliberate surface resemblance and temporal affiliation. I'll accompany her to these places, and so, will be beside her before and after (shared taxi); and throughout, we will be beside ourselves in semblance (shared taxidermy).

Preliminary research reveals that far from being an "ideal" companion (i.e. requiring little to no maintenance), real dolls develop tears during use (the same as bicycle tires). The real doll website offers a silicone patch kit, and so, while the doll is meant to incur a certain amount of handling (rough or otherwise), her body will concretely exhibit the residue of her experience. There is a website detailing real doll surgery, on which is described the nips and tucks such dolls require after hard use.

Real dolls are the product of an assembly line and for all their surface resemblances to an actual human being (female), are meant to be periodically replaced—whether by a process of metonymy—one prosthetic limb for another—or wholesale, the entire doll superceded by another, newer model (human or otherwise).

In the end, I decide that real dolls are, to be blunt, too pretty, too determined to please. I decide to construct my alter-doll out of remaindered medical prostheses and the shop-worn remains of mannequins. Over time, she will be cobbled together out of spare parts, the things that turn up in industrial dumpsters, flea markets and other places I have been rumoured to frequent.

Things I have had in my mouth

Lego block (number five orange).
Dildo.
Vegetable matter.
Fingers.
The abstracted tongues of those I once kissed often, but through circumstance, no longer kiss, and so, even as these recollected tongues are "warm" and "wet," they are imbricated through memory into a single blur of contentment.
Toes.
Penises, clits, pencil stubs.
Traces of rodent fecal matter.
Found mint.
Barbie doll leg.
The extraterrestrial tongues of those I used to love, but in the moment of kissing no longer do.
Nails (human and otherwise).
Involuntary sea-water.
The upright knob of a neo-baroque coffee table.
Utensils.
An elbow, a knee.
Soothers.
The unpremeditated tongues of strangers wearing machine-washable hats.
Canker sores.
Loose teeth.
A near-mint 1972 quarter.
The void tongue of the man I wanted to love, but didn't get to love (as hard as I could have).
Tin foil.
Ice cube.
Vibrating Snoopy tooth brush.
The tongues of those I wanted to and would later love, so that in the moment of kissing, his and her tongue pose long slow inclines into you as moist-lipped strangers contract vertigo at metro stations.
An itinerant pubic hair (possibly my own).
Cavities.

Gobstoppers.

The lubricous hair of strangers routinely found in cafeteria sandwiches.

Tongue depressors.

Dental drills.

Prothodontic tooth.

An impromptu gag.

I saw Dodie Bellamy read a very sexy piece eroticizing a fat man in a flat declamatory voice. Towards the end of the reading (I sat on a couch to the side of the microphone), a tiny drop of spittle had collected at the corner of her mouth. It was wet, *très intime*. I wanted to daub it, collect it, reify it, take it home in a vial and place it in a collection of round and transparent things customarily kept for good luck.

Dr. No would have wondered why Dodie Bellamy just let the spittle lie there, dormant, and didn't work it around in her mouth. In his review of Kiva's *Crème à la Mode*, Dr. No is like: "What about the fun? What about the humour? What about appearing like you enjoy it?" Plus, he's all like, the film is anti-male, just because men don't exist in Kiva's movies (only their cocks): "Don't look for someone grabbing or stroking her hair or breasts or rubbing their cock on her cum-dripping mouth," he goes.

I am familiar with Dr. No from the time I tried to write the novelization of Kiva's *Crème à la Mode*. He kept coming up in the research. I would turn on the VCR and think about Robbes-Grillet—so flat, declamatory—and how, through that surface lens, the repetitive cum shots might look. I would next pop in the film, and while Dr. No prattled on and one video seamlessly led to another, there was no novelization, but a kind of annotated bibliography, an X-rated book of days.

Fuck the kitten (a book of days).

May 5th, 2—

Couleurs de Kiva

I go to Tom's Video to rent a catalogue or video archive of Kiva's orgasms. All the solitary men staring at racks. I wear an oversize pervert coat and a black longshoreman's hat. No one can tell if I am a man or a woman unless they look into my face, but each time someone does, they react. I am given the whole area of the wall I am perusing. The men sidle up and look and shift away, giving me a four foot berth to either side.

May 9th, 2—

Private Castings

I rent *Private Castings* and *The Adjuster*. PC is a series of casting calls for porn. It also depicts photoshoots for their mag, in which the models freeze during intercourse in a slow and deliberate series of gestures. The model extrudes tongue to a clit or a cock, freezing *in situ*. The frenzy comes at the end, when the photos are sped up to catch it all, the sudden phlock-phlock-phlock of the flashbulb as cum strafes the woman's face. They scream: look at the camera, get it in the mouth. And then the woman, mouth open, holds the cum in position waiting for the next penis to be ready. And again. Finally, when they are done, she leans over and ingloriously spits.

May 12, 2—

Gangbang #??

I rent two films: A tri-part gang bang movie (#16, I think) and *Henry Fool*. (I don't get to *Henry Fool*.)

One: A woman parachutes into a field where a chain gang happens to be mulling about. She encourages the men to fuck her, employing the speech patterns of a motivational speaker, like the retired football player on Maury Povich. "C'mon, you bastards, is that all you got?"

Two: View of the mattress as the video store guy holds my hips. Glimpses of a woman wearing a pearl necklace. (A real one). I cum in about two seconds, drop the vibrator and enjoy. The video store guy is holding my hips. Fucking. Pulls out. Takes off the condom and cums on my face.

Three: We detach and lay side by side, commenting on size, shape, technique. Take an interest in oddities and enumerate tissues. The membrane of the blonde's ass distends. Swollen, red. Slightly prolapsed. Now that we've cum, we engage in an academic viewing, cold, clinical.

May 15, 2—

Killer Cumshots #5

In the first scene, the woman is interviewed. She answers the questions politely and with a soft voice, as if applying for the position of hostess. She's asked at one point how many adult movies she's done (answer: about 100 since she got into the business some 2 years ago, having 25 or 30 box covers to her credit). Well, Seamore Snatch tells her, we have a surprise for you tonight. He asks her to get ready for her "surprise." Obedient, her hands move like drugged swans.

Her strokes are graceful, choreographed. And so, look like an unnatural cross between masturbation and synchronized swimming. An exterior sexuality, camera-based. Just when she seems like she might be about to start enjoying herself, Seamore decides her "nipples are hard enough," her "snatch is wet enough," and she is ready, therefore, for her "surprise."

A man named Alex walks into the room.

You can read it on her face: After a hundred adult movies, she thinks, I find myself in a motel with a man named Seamore Snatch who has a video camera and a shotgun assistant with a still camera and the surprise is? A man to fuck, oh yeah, *quelle surprise*. Before Alex enters, anything is possible. Maybe Seamore bought her a miniature horse or a lollipop. Once, my gynecologist, who hired me to write personalized porn for her husband, gave me a silver-foil wrapped box, and in it, a present. It could have been anything. Not even size was a determinant, because the silver box could have contained directions to a much bigger box.

The silver box reminded me of Wilhelm Reich and also, a beef bullion cube. I loved the box, like Pandora, like Schrödinger. I have never, to this day, opened it. Instead, I gave it into the care of a friend, sworn to never tell me the contents.

And so, I feel her disappointment.

They move through the usual series of positions. The preliminary orals: him on her; her on him. Tongues extruded, they move into missionary, doggie, woman on top, straddle-spread for the camera. And then a spooning anal scene—where, oddly, the original audio is over-dubbed with asynchronous moans, but as it is single camera work and her face is apparent, you can still read her lips. She's saying: "Hey asshole, you ever heard of lube?"

I fast forward a couple of scenes. A woman. Her gestures sluggish, her features coalescing into grotesque caricatures of pleasure. I eject the tape a little prematurely to watch Kiva again. Later, I will bring myself to orgasm in the bathroom while watching in a hand-held mirror. Dispel drowsy wrists with commonplace convulsions.

TODD SWIFT

NOTE TO THE EDITOR

This poem is from a long series
on the life of the man who invented dirigibles
whose name is French, or Hungarian
I think. Dietrich Katona?

Note that
I am using a special font here—Strontium Victorian—
and you must make certain to keep the size at 7.2
and also capitalize all the names of fish,
except if freshwater.

The sequence on the invention of dice has been suppressed pending an investigation.

***

All the place names in the Confession Poems should be deleted,
to be replaced with Xs and long dashes.

Please fact-check my biography.

Wyoming is spelled "Wyoming" and yes, I am that old.

"Hypo-allergenic" has a dash.

You might be intrigued to note that I am the winner of the following international
poetry competitions and prizes:
1. THE WALDO VINCENT MEMORIAL HAIKU CONTEST;
2. MS. EUNICE HALIBURTON CHAPBOOK PRIZE FOR BEST FOURTH CHAP-
BOOK;
3. THE UNIVERSITY OF TANZANIA'S INTERNATIONAL SONNET CONTEST;
4. UNESCO PRIZE FOR BEST VEGETABLE POEM;
5. JAKE'S AUTOBODY BIANNUAL FIRST BOOK AWARD;
6. DR. AND MRS. RADNOTI'S ONE AND ONLY TOP POEM CHOICE;
7. DATGEIST'S BEST, 1970.

The following poems have appeared
in *NO POSSIBLE WAY; NEW AND FAIRLY RECENT LINES;*
GODSQUAWK; ERGOMATIC; SUNSHINE STATE MARGINALIA;
CORPUS GUSSY; THE TROUBADOUR LIVES!; SKELETAL AFFLATUS;
BONGO CONGO MONGO; DELIRIUM TREMENDOUS; DATGEIST;
MR. FRIENDLY; MY NAME IS PETE AND I AM BI; ONLY TWICE;
LAST PETROL STATION FOR A HUNDRED MILES; ZOOMER.

You are welcome to choose any of the poems
but I would strongly suggest you choose the following:
"i am not in favour of capital punishment"; "burning dolls, watering cans";
"elegy for a dead amnesiac"; "seven ways of adjusting a corset";
"the years following 1798, especially 1816, 1909 and 1972";
"gadzooks! Why I Smoke Such Good Cigars" and "NO WOMEN CAN DO
THE DANCE LIKE A MAN ENTRANCED" (please note the caps).

My name should be spelled in full, including all titles.
My photo is not included, but is available upon request
from the Department of Justice.

Thank you for your interest in my work, which
means a lot to me and my seven brothers,
who live near you, and are karate experts.
Don't be shy to tell me what you think.
Praise Jesus!

And thank you once again. This is the only anthology
I have been asked to submit to.
Submit is such a funny word, isn't it?

I hope the poems on the death of tubercular infants
do not offend you. My sisters had this disease
and it is based on actual experience "recollected
in solitude" but you know how it goes.
Okay, I may have made some of it up.
But the pus on the collar is actually true.

I saw that.

I think the name may be Dieter Kazner.
I'll get back to you on that.

By the way, did you have a chance to check my poetry
web site: www.allfatgirlsconstantly.com?
It is not a sex site, don't worry. He he.

I am very interested in the photographs of your wife
on your site. Is she really that size?

Thank you again and send me a reply in six to seven hours
so I can tell the people I live with all about it.
I hope I won't have to put my disappointment hat
on today.

Yours, cheers, all the best, thank you, felicitations, *au revoir*, a river derci, signing off
for now, have a good week-end, and much appreciated,

Des Katboy

PS: This is a nom de plume. My real name is different. It is Desmond Kattman Jr.,
but what do you think of Katboy? It makes me think of cats. It gets lots of 'lovely
ladies' interested at open mics.

PPS: I am not a SPOKEN WORD PERFORMANCE POET! I am a poet, plain and
simple.

DK

cc: Mr. & Mrs. Desmond Kattman

IRON MAN

A man called Dick from the US of A drags his quadriplegic nonverbal son Rick through the Germany Iron Man, the biggest triathlon in Europe. And as he's hauling his son and his son's rubber dingy out of the river they're blasting "O Fortuna" from a temporary radio tower. And the Germans are being driven to tears to madness to tears to the music and I am the only one, of 200,000 spectators, who laughs. And I laugh because it's like TV the way I always laugh when something's like TV like when you run into your closest friend at a bookstore neither of you have ever been to before, or you make out in a park in the rain. And so laughing seems appropriate, and the Germans' tears seem fake and manipulated, sort of eked out, like they're acting.

Why hadn't Rick been asked if he would like to do the triathlon? Why did no one ask him what he would like to do on the weekend? That's what a girl A NUT asked Dick. On the telephone. And after Dick hung up, Dick's wife Crystal said "Leave it alone Dick." Just leave it alone and come to bed, you can't account for nuts like that, you know you're a good man. And instead, Dick sat up and drank. One beer after another like it was highschool and Barry Butcher was watching like he was gonna be called a pussy if he didn't drink the whole goddamn case if he didn't drink the whole goddamn world, and he thought about what that bitch had said. He *had* asked Rick if he would like to do a triathlon. And that was what made him sit up and drink beer. And play on his computer. And while he was playing on his computer he noticed for the first time that when he poked the soft screen of his laptop with his two index fingers, the screen looked, for about a second and a half, like a negative of a photo of two perfect breasts. With half-erect nipples. He did it a few times. About a dozen times. And he thought about how he knew that. He knew something that complex and he was not that wise a man. And when he asked Rick, his son, if he would like to do a triathlon, he asked it the same way he asks his closet "where are you blue sweater?" or his dog "how are ya buddy?"

Dick is still drinking. To this very second. To *this* very second. Beer after beer after beer after beer. On a nightly basis Crystal tells him to come to bed and on a nightly basis Dick pokes the soft screen of his laptop till it's obsolete, till it's been obsolete for years, till there's like fourteen computers out there he could buy that are better than the one he's poking and he drinks beer after beer after beer and slowly but surely his legs turn soft and mushy where they were triathlon hard and his chest kind of folds in where it was made of pure brawn. And the more he thinks about the negative photo of the two breasts with the half-erect nipples the more he feels like a chump, and when you feel like a chump you don't feel much like talking to anybody cause it feels like a lie, so he stops. He stops talking to Crystal to Rick to the dog even to the goddamn closet and they miss him. But they know he's had it rough, they know that he's good, he's just being stoic, he is, after all, an Iron Man. A very special kind of Iron Man, gave his quadriplegic non-verbal unfortunate pitiable son something most of us could never dream of. And Rick's learning things in physio, really making progress, new techniques, focus on economical movement to reduce spasm. Crystal tells him every night before she goes to bed all about it, and then the dog tells him one more time before *he* hits the hay, but poor Dick's too fucking hammered to notice that his dog just talked.

THERE IS SOMETHING ABOUT EUROPE AND YEAST INFECTIONS

There is something about Europe and yeast infections. I remember reading an excerpt from a novel when I was maybe fifteen about a woman travelling through France with her fiancée and rather than describe France as I had hoped it would, the passage detailed the woman's nightly routine of soaking maxi pads in buttermilk. This cure caused her underpants to make squishing noises.

It is especially demeaning to be naked only from the waist down. I have been told to take off my pants, which I do, and I stand in the tiny curtained-off dressing room in my tank top, my socks and my sandals. My overalls lie in a heap beside me. No one in Germany wears socks with sandals. No one in Germany wears overalls. I feel like an asshole. I look in the mirror and think of Donald Duck. What in God's name is the point of this dressing room I think as I head into the examining room, nervously holding my overalls in front of me, trying to play it cool, trying not to look like the Canadian prude that I am. Upon entry I note that "Student Hospital" must be a continental euphemism for torture chamber. The doctor smiles and invites me to have a seat. In the metal chair with handles and stirrups. Thank you. I was always under the impression that one could tell a doctor, regardless of the language, it itches…down there, a prescription would be written, you'd be told to eat yoghurt, you'd trundle off to the pharmacy singing. Instead my fists sweat around the metal handles, my feet visibly shake inside their socks, sandals and stirrups, the speculum drawer is opened and the med student who is apparently learning something from my public humiliation selects a shiny little number about the size of an English cucumber.

"You've had children, yes?"

"No." I begin to breathe again as the student selects a slightly smaller model.

"But you've had *Geschlechtsverkehr*." The word means sex but the direct translation is gender traffic.

"No."

The student hands the doctor a puny little speculum and the drawer is closed. My pride is strangely wounded.

Just when I think it's all over, the med student is invited to smell the speculum and make a guess at what ails me. And I'm still not wearing any pants. After a good sniff, the med student diagnoses me with a yeast infection and I learn a new word in German. *Pilzkrankung*. Fabulous. I go to the pharmacy, get a box of suppositories that I have to keep in the fridge that I share with four people I barely know, and arrive home to my dorm to discover that there is no applicator included. Just some little condoms for my fingers.

That's a most remarkable story says my ridiculous sister, to whom I only tell such things so she'll tell me they're remarkable and I can yell at her that she's ridiculous.

"Finger condoms, Amber. Little condoms for my fingers."

"Remarkable."

"Is Dad home?"

The phone connection is bad today, there's a weird little echo and I hear my own voice whine back at me, every word I say.

My father would like to know if I have enough money, what I've been eating, if I've registered for my student visa yet and my phone card runs out of money before I can finish saying I love you.

"I lo—"

I'm certain he thinks "I lo—st my passport" and I walk along the cobbled street feeling itchy and alien.

SPOILT

He is told to stop asking questions before he gets killed. He didn't find a clone, he is the clone. That's another him, from the future. He is a replicant. He is an impostor. He had his body frozen until his condition could be treated. He faked his death with the help of a doctor whom he then killed. We don't know if the crimes are real, or in his imagination.

He is the son of the sheriff who raped his mom and he was seeking revenge. He is his own father. They're actually the same person. He killed him because he had fallen in love with him. He was being double-crossed by the people who hired him. One of the hundreds of anonymous papers he processed in the course of his daily work happened to be the one bit of evidence that could link the perpetrators of an embezzlement scheme to the crime and even though he has no memory of that he was poisoned anyway. The correct antibody was available but never tried. His death was faked with the help of a stuntman. They killed him to cover up their own cowardice. He set up the car accident to boost his own career. He was God all along. He rigs the car to try to kill him. The snuff film is real. He is actually wearing a bulletproof vest. His daughter has the Gift too. He saves the President, but destroys the tape that would bring about world peace.

They're all delusions. He kills everyone. His therapist is the killer. The videotapes show the murders. It's all part of a dream that he is having. He inadvertently proves his involvement in the attempted murder of his wife by letting himself into his apartment using the key he hid for the killer. She is not really dead, but head of the FBI team in charge of the investigation into the murders. They kill all the bad cops. He chooses to become human, but then she dies in a car accident. Stricken with guilt, he reveals himself during the shoot-out and gets shot in the head. The transfer student is the Queen alien and after they kill her, everyone returns to normal.

She's in on the plan to rob the bank. He rescues her but she was sent to kill him. She set him up, having swapped identities with a high school friend. She is seducing all the other patients. The effects of the drug are temporary, and the patients revert to their original state. She is the killer. She's a man. She is real and not an imaginary friend. She's not an orphan. She wasn't even involved in the orgy, but did it all to prove a point. She had tied herself up to force her father to deal with her rape. She blames the death of her mother on the neighbours. She is the girl's sister and her mother. She really was talking to God. She was dying of cancer anyway, and goaded him into killing her to load him up with guilt. She's not the killer—it's her ex, who is now stalking every man she dates. She is actually the killer—her missing ex who threatens to kill her is in her imagination—she killed him months ago. The last wish is used for someone else's happiness. She gets the guy. She kills him, making it look like a case of self-defense. As he is ready to commit suicide to donate his own heart, they learn that another donor has been found. She returns back in time to be with him.

The rooms are moving. He is also a transvestite. He, disguised as a woman, is the killer. He is captured and beheaded. The boy feeds the girl to the dog. His wife's head is in the box. His rescue is a dream. He wakes up to find his head attached to her body. She killed him and disposed of him in the BBQ. His friend hired the one-armed man to kill him and his wife in order to cover up his medical fraud. He's the one who actually killed his wife, and is chasing the killer to block out the memory of it. There is no actual dog—he is insane and believes he is a dog. She recaptures him but pairs him with an escape artist for his transport back to prison. There is no twin brother—he has multiple personality disorder. It was all a birthday present in the end. He didn't abandon her—he loved her till the end. They're actually brother and sister. He created the ghosts to scare away other prospectors. She set up her boyfriend to kill her father for his land. He killed their parents so he could adopt them and use their inheritance to pay off a loan shark. He robbed his own office. His illegitimate son killed him. Handcuffed to her, he slices off his own hand to escape. The girls win the pageant. They kill her mother and the police find the diaries. The house is in fact alive, and invited the guests itself.

He wakes up from the dream of his death and repents. He is actually the director of the asylum where they are being held. He's still married to the madwoman hidden in the upstairs room. The kids telling the stories are all actually dead. The car accident is revealed to be much worse than it seemed. He is shot and killed by a punk he had a run-in with earlier. They kill each other as the house collapses around them. They agree that they love each other but cannot be together. He decides he wants to live. He survives the night only to be impaled by the gate when he tries to leave at dawn. He fell to his death, but as they leave, they notice his body is missing. The killer escapes by substituting a dead body in the driver's seat and running the truck off the cliff. He doesn't really kill himself, he just let them think that. He is the same man she saved in the car accident at the beginning. They are both aliens. They are actually angels. Nobody is actually killed.

He really did kill all those people. Both him and his wife are alien impostor android bombs. They are the last two people left on earth. The ship has been in Hell and is now killing everybody. He is the only survivor. They're unable to return to the present with the ship. They find out that they haven't escaped yet. He's already dead—everything that happens is part of his refusal to accept his own death. He had stayed behind, detonating the explosives manually, saving the planet. He is acquitted of the bombing. The ghosts that were haunting them are actually living people who are attempting to have them exorcised. He calls the demon, thus becoming the demon for the next man to call.

They've never left the Matrix. The machine has the power to turn thoughts into reality. The monster is the product of his imagination. They trick it onto holy ground where it dies. It is made of people. They are left alive on the ground as the headhunters close in. The contents of the briefcase are never revealed.

VOODOO

It is Wednesday, March 10, 1999
and Gail Cheshire, brown-haired with
blue eyes, a pretty girl by anyone's standards,
lives at 76 Buckingham Ave. in Toronto, Ontario.
The postal code is M4N 1R4.
Her phone number is (416) 920-9741.
You can call her or write her a letter.
She may be amused and invite you over,
or be frightened enough by your solicitation
to call the police.

She has a sister named Maeve.
They both attend Branksome Hall,
an upper-class private school just off
Mount Pleasant Rd. in the heart of
Toronto's wealthiest neighbourhood.
A beautiful school by anyone's standards.

At 10 Elm Ave., Branksome Hall spans both
sides of the road, surrounded by green
trees and bountiful bushes. You can attend
Branksome as well if you are a young girl
living in Toronto, whose parents are
willing to spend $11,995 CAN
per year on your education.

By the time you read this,
Gail Cheshire may not be living
at this address. Maybe the phone
number will have been changed. Maybe
she will have gone off to the university
or college of her choice. Maybe she'll
have a boyfriend, or a girlfriend.

Maybe some calamity will have entered the lives
of the Cheshire household. Maybe her dad who's a doctor
will be found too late with a tumour in his brain.
Maybe bad things happen to good people.

Maybe dirty boys and dirty girls are calling her
up and telling her astonishing things. Maybe she
is receiving a lot of mail. Maybe she will become
a cult celebrity without knowing why. Maybe she will
blame herself. Maybe she will be kidnapped by a
crazed and obsessed fan. Maybe she will be found
on his shrine to her. Maybe someone has taken her
picture and stolen her soul. Maybe she really feels
way too open right now.

TREASURE HUNT

Hello. I am a 48 yr. old MWM, 5'11", 160lbs, dirty blond hair, blue eyes, have a nice build, am fun to be with and financially secure from the Burlington area. I am a passionate music-lover and I have diverse musical tastes. I cook, am down-to-earth, spontaneous, intelligent and outgoing. I am looking to spend some time with my daughter, Sarah, shopping, basketball and so on. She is a SWF aged 15, 5'6", about 120lbs, very pretty, brown hair, blue eyes, slight build and a recreational smoker. Enjoys painting, rowing and museums. Avid collector of butterflies. She has been missing since Nov. 15, 1998, disappearing after school. Last seen wearing a St. Mary's school green uniform kilt (MacInnes Clan tartan) $45, St. Mary's blouse $25, school sweater $80, Club Monaco brown suede jacket $180, dark blue tights by Hanes $6, and Aldo loafers $120. She is possibly in the company of Jay Thomas Porter. D.O.B: Oct.13, 1974, eye colour: brown, hair colour: dark brown with bright red streaks. A sharp gentleman who knows his way around the city and needs a classy-looking woman to share unforgettable times. Distinguishing features: a gothic Celtic band resembling barbed wire around his right bicep. **Call 1-800-387-7962** toll-free if you have any information about this missing child. For the Club Monaco retail outlet nearest you, call **1-800-528-7228. Call 212-752-7822 EXT 8194** ($1.95 per min.) to respond to this ad and leave a personal message. All calls are confidential.

WHAT'S WITH THE BOWTIE, JIMBO?

Does it make you feel more Conservative, more
in charge, more like a manly man? Do you wear it
to bed over two pairs of jammies to get your wife
all lukewarm and bothered? Does she call you her
            beeg stud moofan?

Do you know what a dingleberry is, Jim? Dingleberries
are the hardened balls of poo that dangle from the wool
            around a sheep's anus.

And what's with the new Jag when the profits are down
and the industry's in a tailspin, Jim? And what's with you
being a complete fucking cocksucker asshole, I wonder?
Will that be explained in the biweekly newsletter about
            your whole prestigious famn damily?

Know what, Jim? I like you. I like that a man of your station
still has the conviction to send his secretary home because
her skirt hem is one indecent inch above her knees, and I like
that your bowtie makes you look like a wiener, and that men
such as you call to mind such deliciously descriptive words as
            dingleberry, which I don't get to use very often.

THE PURPLE NURPLE

There is nothing else in nature so effective,
        a tornado of seizures
bound in a knuckle. It's easy:

        simply pinch the nipple
between the thumb and pointy finger
        and wrench it around
four hundred degrees or so.

Yes, child, the flesh *is* weak. See,
        the resulting bruise
takes the shape of mini-sunbursts.

The nipple is where the nerves have built
        little balconies into the world
from which to expose themselves.

Ask a nipple if it knows the feel of gravel
        embedded in the skin.
Now ask your knees.

        Primate behaviour
has unaccounted for variations.
        For instance: young male
        chimpanzees will
wrestle and fight and punch and
        bite to establish dominance,

much in the way of adolescent boys,
        but for some reason
our cousins the apes have not included
the purple nurple in their rituals—

perhaps they're not evolved enough.

Ask Calvin Little, age 13,
        breathless on his knees
in the gravel, crying uncle,
if he doesn't believe it takes a certain
amount of logic and reasoning
          to conceive of torture.

Rural Elementary

Jamie Lyle was playing circus by the turkey crates,
tightrope walking, holding a mop handle for balance,
when he fell into a vat of liquid manure and drowned,
so Mr. Palmer the principal called Father Borghese
to come our school and tell us why we die,
and reassure us that Jamie had been baptized
and wasn't going to Hell.

Kevin Vranic was lucky; Kevin tumbled
off the back of his dad's tractor, lost an arm
and missed the rest of grade three.
When he came back he had to get up on stage
to talk about his accident, and the whole school
gathered round to watch Kevin pick up a pencil,
opening and closing the hook on his new arm
by flexing a muscle in his shoulder.

He had to take it off to play soccer; that hook
could hurt someone, rip someone's shorts, poke
someone's eye out, and Scott Hague and Dave Skinner
got suspended for throwing the arm into a tree,
but Kevin climbed to the top and got it down—
all by himself.

SHERI-D WILSON

SPINSTERS HANGING IN TREES:
VESTIR SANTOS

From high in a tree,
over the hill,
not so far, from Spinsterville,
perched on one knee,
I pop the question: extraordinary-
Will you marry me?
Of course.
It will mean you have to compromise.
How can I compromise myself?

At what age do you become, a 'SPINSTER'?

We are the Spinsters hanging in trees,
hanging in trees—at 45 degrees.
We are the black holes, with no line after us-
the women who've never wed.
At us is where the line stops,
dead. Old vacuum cleaner bags.
Oh yes.
There's one in every family.
Bone crones covered in stigma and sags.

NASTY

Eccentric single aunts, who spoil their cats and dogs and birds,
from their paltry little rooms and thatched roofed houses.
Ugly, crusty, lonely, barren: infertilians.
Wrinkled, dried-up, shrivelled washed-up: infertilians, with warts and facial hair.
Broken down jalopies *sans* a spare. Disintegrating twigs
in sand shoes, the crypto-relic shrews,
with painted on eye brows and old lady perfume.
Left hanging in trees, at 45 degrees.
Looking petrified. Like poster girls of a degenerative disease,
mummified. The belles without a ring.

143

SNAP!
Old Maid's become a new parlour game
NOW

We are the Neo-Spinsters
Spin-masters, spin-misters, spin-sisters
Spinning
With monkeys and motorcycles
Surf boards and string bikinis
With shaved heads and tattooed shoulders
Gold credit and trips around the world
-uptown downbeat, uptown downbeat-
Snappy spinster girls

We're the confetti escapers
Doin' it for ourselves

JUICY

We are the Neo-Spinsters
Springs in trees
With the spider monkeys and the birds and the bees
In the trees
We're butterflies perched in protest
We're Luna with black-belted keys
Oh yes
We are hanging in the brittle boned forests of families of trees
We are the eyes of the witches that rustle high in their branches

I am the happy Spinster
Broom outside my door

According to the Times
I have more, testosterone
Women who never marry
Are harmoniously scary

SCARY

I am the happy Spinster
Broom outside my door

He asked my father for my hand in marriage
We had the dress, the shoes, the carriage
The rings, and the church
When I said:
"I'm not gonna iron your shirts"
He had a fit
So when we split
I told him to return my hand to my father
Matrimony manikin part
And I went to my father
And I asked if I could have my own hand and heart
To have and to hold and to hang
'Till death do I
I do
Do I?
Do

INFELIX DIDO

We are the Neo-Spinsters
We didn't make our bed
We made our leer jet
And now
We're just gonna have to fly in it

ON BEING A POET

Relationships are good for at least two poems:
One at the beginning
And one at the end

AUTHOR BIOS

ROBERT ALLEN is a novelist and poet. His most recent books are *Ricky Ricardo Suites* (poems) and *Napoleon's Retreat*, a novel, both published by DC Books, Montreal. His long poem, *The Encantadas*, will appear in 2003 with Signal Editions, Véhicule Press, Montreal. He is the editor of the literary review *Matrix*.

RYAN ARNOLD has been destined to fail since his unassuming birth in a Vancouver hospital hallway in 1978. In accordance with his forthcoming demise, he writes fiction, poetry, and droll whatnot. He is a graduate of Concordia University and has successfully botched opportunities with Tony Gwynn-like consistency. His writing has been hailed as "spiteful," "petty tripe," and the "Wrestlemania of crap."

JOE BLADES is not just a poet with three books, a score of chapbooks, and contributions to numerous anthologies and periodicals. He is an editor and the publisher of Broken Jaw Press, a visual artist who graduated from the Nova Scotia College of Art and Design (BFA 1988), and a community radio producer at CHSR 97.9 FM with the weekly *Ashes, Paper & Beans: Fredericton's Poetry & Writing Show*. Blades is the editor of several books including *Jive Talk: George Fetherling in Interviews and Documents* and *Great Lakes Logia*, both published in 2001. His poetry books are *Cover Makes a Set* (1990), *River Suite* (1998) and *Open Road West* (2000, 2001).

ANDY BROWN, 24, lives in Phoenix and designs cool street wear for the people everyone wants to be. He says that since 1999, his "Soldier Leisure" T-shirts, hoodies and beanies have appealed to men and women who are thinking for themselves—individuals and trendsetters. "My clothes are more design-intense rather than logo-intense. Rocking a big logo sucks. That's why, on my hoodies, the big logo is upside down."

STEPHEN CAIN is the author of *dyslexicon* (Coach House, 1999) and *Torontology* (ECW Press, 2001) as well as numerous chapbooks and broadsides. His sound poetry can be heard on *Carnivocal* (Red Deer, 1999) and his visual poetry has appeared in such magazines as *Rampike*, *Torque*, and *Essex*. He operates the micropress Kitsch in Ink and is a literary editor at the *Queen Street Quarterly*. Born in 1970, Stephen Cain lives in Toronto.

JASON CAMLOT is a Montreal-born poet, songwriter and critic. He is the author of *The Animal Library* (DC Books, 2000), recently nominated for the Quebec Writer's Federation A.M. Klein prize for poetry. He teaches Romantic and Victorian literature at Concordia University, and plays bass guitar in the rawk outfit Puggy Hammer.

MARGARET CHRISTAKOS is a Sudbury-born, Toronto-bound (since 1987) writer of poetry and prose. Her most recent book publications are *Charisma*, a 2000 novel short-listed for Ontario's Trillium Book Award, and *Excessive Love Prostheses*, a collection of poetry from Coach House Books released in 2002. Her previous poetry collections are: *Wipe Under A Love* (The Mansfield Press, 2000), *The Moment Coming* (ECW Press, 1998), *Other Words For Grace* (Mercury Press, 1994), and *Not Egypt* (Coach House Press, 1989, now online at www.chbooks.com). Her poems have been called "something else." She reads many fairytales to her three kids, sometimes *ad delirium*.

JON PAUL FIORENTINO: 5'11. 195 lbs. Shoots: Right. Born: Winnipeg MB, 1975.

COREY FROST was born in P.E.I., his passport says, and he is currently living under a bridge next to the East River in New York, but he still persists in saying he is "from" Montreal. He writes about the immanence of language, the impossibility of truth, and then eats a sandwich. The sandwich is okay, but the slices of turkey within the sandwich are not real. They're fake. The turkey is not real turkey; it's artificial. It's not "tofurkey" mind you. But it is made of something other than turkey. "A note about the author's name" is from his book *My Own Devices* (conundrum press, 2002).

VALERIE JOY KALYNCHUK is a founding member of Murmurs of Nose.

RYAN KAMSTRA is a poet, songwriter and make-out artist currently (& not for much longer) based in Toronto. He has an album *aLL fALL dOWN* (2001, independent) and a book of poetry *lATE cAPITALIST sUBLIME* (2002, Insomniac Press).

DAVID MCGIMPSEY's most recent collection of poetry is *Hamburger Valley, California* (ECW Press). He is also a member of the rock band Puggy Hammer. He teaches creative writing at Concordia University.

ROB MCLENNAN lives in Ottawa, even though he was born there once. A prolific writer, etc., his 8th full-length poetry collection is *red earth* (Black Moss), & he is editor of the anthologies *side/lines: a new canadian poetics* (Insomniac Press) & *Groundswell: best of above/ground press*, 1993-2003 (cauldron books / Broken Jaw Press). Despite being currently single, he considers himself the most beautiful straight man in Ottawa.

NATHANIEL G. MOORE was born in Toronto in 1974 and grew up in East York. His work has appeared in *This Magazine*, *b+a new fiction*, *The Antigonish Review* and *Front & Centre*. His debut novel about the Roman poet Catullus is forthcoming with Coach House Books in Spring 2004.

EVA MORAN graduated with an English Honours degree from Glendon College. She is an M.A. student at Concordia University. After this publication, Eva WILL NEVER WRITE AGAIN!

HAL NIEDZVIECKI is editor of *Broken Pencil*, the magazine of zine culture and the independent arts (www.brokenpencil.com). His work of cultural criticism, *We Want Some Too: Underground Desire and the Reinvention of Mass Culture* was published by Penguin Canada in Spring 2000. In Fall 2001, Random House Canada published Hal's novel *Ditch*, a coming of age cyber-porn thriller.

MARK PATERSON is a Montreal writer whose short fiction has appeared in *Pagitica*, *Blood + Aphorisms*, *Sub-TERRAIN*, *Broken Pencil*, and the anthology *Telling Stories: New English Fiction from Quebec* (Véhicule Press, 2002). Publications are also forthcoming in *The Lichen Journal*, *Metropole*, the anthology *Island Dreams* (Véhicule Press), and the spoken word CD anthology *Dubref: Session II*. Mark produces and co-hosts The Grimy Windows Variety Showcase, a monthly series at Hurley's Irish Pub featuring writers, poets, musicians, comedians, filmmakers, and wrestlers. He is currently working on a novel about worker's compensation and alien abductions.

JAMIE POPOWICH is currently peddling monkeys to the locals.

ROBERT PRIEST is widely adored as the 2nd best poet in Canada. These poems are from *Resurrection in the Cartoon* (ECW Press). Visit his website at www.poempainter.com.

STUART ROSS has been active in the Toronto literary scene for over 25 years. He sold 7,000 copies of his self-published chapbooks in the streets of Toronto during the '80s, has edited several literary magazines—most recently *Peter O'Toole*—and is co-founder of the Toronto Small Press Fair. A prolific writer, performer, editor, and teacher, he has read at hundreds of venues in Canada, the U.S., the U.K., and Nicaragua. His work has appeared in scores of journals here and in the U.S., including *Harper's, This Magazine, Geist, Rampike* and *Bomb Threat Checklist*. His recent books include *Henry Kafka & Other Stories* (The Mercury Press) and the poetry collections *Farmer Gloomy's New Hybrid* (ECW Press), which was shortlisted for the 2000 Trillium Award, *Razovsky at Peace* (ECW Press) and *Hey, Crumbling Balcony! Poems New & Selected* (ECW Press). Stuart's online residence is www.hunkamooga.com.

VICTORIA STANTON is a performance artist based in Montreal. Presented text-based / visual performance and videos in Canada, the U.S. and Europe. Spoken word recordings on various CD compilations, and broadcast on regional and national radio. Artist-books exhibited in group shows in Canada and across the U.S. Co-author with Vincent Tinguely of *Impure: Reinventing the Word* (conundrum press, 2001). Performance and critical texts published in Canadian / American anthologies and art / literary magazines. www.bankofvictoria.com

SARAH STEINBERG lives and works in Montreal but dreams of one day living in Dorval. She can be seen weeknights on the popular TV series *Touched by an Angel*.

ANNE STONE is the author of the chapbook *sweet dick all*, and the novels *jacks: a gothic gospel,* and *Hush*. She has published poetry and fiction in numerous literary magazines, journals, and chapbooks.

TODD SWIFT is a Montreal-born poet, anthologist, essayist, screenwriter, and cultural activist. He is the author or an editor of six books, including *100 Poets Against The War* (Salt, 2003) and his most recent collection of poems, *Cafe Alibi* (DC Books, 2002). He recently released a CD on the Wired On Words label, *The Envelope, Please,* as Swifty Lazarus (with Tom Walsh). He has read or emceed at hundreds of literary venues, from the Dylan Thomas Centre in Swansea, to the New School in New York. From 1998-2001 he was visiting lecturer at Budapest University (ELTE). Swift is a contributing editor for *Matrix* magazine, and poetry editor of London-based online journal Nthposition.com. His writing appears in *The National Post, Literary Review of Canada, en Route, Jacket, Poetry Wales* and *The Dubliner,* among other places. He lives in Paris.

JULIA TAUSCH goes to school in Montreal. Her work has been published in *Matrix* and *The Cyclops Review*. She also has a chapbook called *Gepacktrager*. Her first novel is entitled *Another Book About Another Broken Heart* (conundrum press, 2003). She is a big fan of eating and love.

SHERWIN TJIA is a Montreal-based poet and painter. Books include *Gentle Fictions* (poems) and *Pedigree Girls* (comix). Work can be seen in *Queen Street Quarterly, Crank, dig, Quarry, Adbusters, Wegway, Kiss Machine, Trucker, Geist, Lit. Review of Canada, The New Irregular* and the *Serialist Manifesto.* To get the books, go to www.insomniacpress.com. For more sordid details, go to www.pedigreegirls.com. To contact him directly, email pedigreegirls@hotmail.com.

PAUL VERMEERSCH is a Toronto-based poet and editor of Insomniac Press's new poetry imprint *4:AM Books*. His poems have appeared in journals and magazines in Canada, the U.S., and Europe. His first full-length collection of poems *Burn* (ECW Press, 2000) was a finalist for the 2001 Gerald Lampert Memorial Award for the best English language poetic debut in Canada. In 1998 he founded the I.V. Lounge Reading Series, where he continues to curate and host readings on a regular basis. His anthology *The I.V. Lounge Reader* (Insomniac Press) was published in 2001 to critical acclaim. His most recent poetry collection is *The Fat Kid* (ECW Press, 2002).

SHERI-D WILSON is a distinguished poet, playwright, performer, essayist and teacher, often called "The Mama of Dada." Her unparalleled performance style is rich with erotic jazz, infused with a sharp feminist sensibility, and laced with dangerous wit.

Publication Notes

Allen, Robert. *Ricky Ricardo Suites*. Montreal: DC Books, 2000.

Blades, Joe. *Open RoadWest*. Fredericton: Broken Jaw Press, 1999.

Brown, Andy. *The Andy Brown Project*. Montreal: conundrum press, 2002.

Christakos, Margaret. *Excessive Love Prostheses*. Toronto: Coach House Books, 2002.

Frost, Corey. *My Own Devices*. Montreal: conundrum press, 2002.

Kalynchuk, Valerie Joy. *All Day Breakfast*. Montreal: conundrum press, 2001.

mclennan, rob. *Harvest: A Book of Signifiers*. Vancouver: Talon, 2001.

———. *Paper Hotel*. Fredericton: Broken Jaw Press, 2002.

Priest, Robert. *Resurrection in the Cartoon*. Toronto: ECW Press, 2003.

Ross, Stuart. "The President's Cold Legs." *Canadian Forum*.

———. *Me and the Pope*. Toronto: Proper Tales Press, 2002.

Steinberg, Sarah. "Kindergarten Art Critiques." *Matrix*, 63. Illustrations by Malin Holmquist.

Stone, Anne. "Real Doll." *Matrix*, 62.

Tjia, Sherwin. *Gentle Fictions*. Toronto: Insomniac, 2001.

Vermeersch, Paul. *The Fat Kid*. Toronto: ECW Press/A MisFit Book, 2002.

———. *Burn*. Toronto: ECW Press/A MisFit Book, 2000.

———. *Time to Kill Boss*. Toronto: Dwarf Puppets on Parade/a division of Proper Tales Press, 2002.

Wilson, Sheri-D. *Between Lovers*. Vancouver: Arsenal Pulp Press, 2002.